These Hawaii Golf Courses Offer Great Variety, From Mountain Tops To Oceanside. And With The American Express® Card You Can Play Them All.

MAUI

HAWAII

Don't Leave Home Without It.®

ISLAND OF HAWAII
Alii Country Club
Hapuna Golf Course
Kona Country Club
Mauna Kea Beach Golf Course
Mauna Lani Resort
Sea Mountain Golf Course
Waikaloa Golf Club - Beach Course
Waikaloa Golf Club - Kings' Course
Waikaloa Village Golf Club
Volcano Golf and Country Club
Naniloa Country Club

ISLAND OF MAUI
Kaanapali Golf Courses
Kapalua Golf Club - Bay Course
Kapalua Golf Course - Village Course
Kapalua Golf Club - Plantation Course
Makena Golf Club
Wailea Golf Club - Blue Course
Wailea Golf Club - Gold Course
Waikapu Valley Country Club

ISLAND OF LANAI
The Experience at Koele
The Challenge at Manele

ISLAND OF MOLOKAI
Kaluakoi Golf Course

ISLAND OF OAHU
Hawaii Prince Golf Club
Ko Olina Golf Club
Turtle Bay Hilton and Country Club
Hawaii Kai Golf Courses
Makaha Valley Country Club
Mililani Golf Club
Olomana Golf Links
Pearl Country Club
Honolulu Country Club
Royal Hawaiian County Club
Koolau Golf Course
Waikele Golf Club
Barbers Point Golf Course

ISLAND OF KAUAI
Kauai Lagoons Resort
Kiahuna Golf Club
Poipu Bay Resort Golf Course
Princeville - Makai Golf Course
Princeville - Prince Golf and Country Club

©1994 American Express Travel Related Services Company, Inc.

GOLF HAWAII

Table of Contents

Aloha from the Islands 3

MAUI
Aloha Maui 4
Kapalua Golf Club 6
Kaanapali Golf Courses 12
Wailea Golf Course 14
Maui Country Club 15
Silversword Golf Club 15
Makena Golf Course 16
Pukalani Country Club 19
Sandalwood Golf Course 20
Grand Waikapu Golf Course 20
Waiehu Municipal Golf Course 21

OAHU
Aloha Oahu 22
Hawaii Prince Golf Club 25
Sheraton Makaha Resort & Country Club 26
Mid Pacific Country Club 29
Makaha Valley Country Club 29
Koolau Golf Course 30
Royal Hawaiian Golf Club 35
Ko Olina Golf Club & Resort 36
Ala Wai Municipal Golf Course 38
The Links at Kuilima 40
Turtle Bay Country Club 40
Pearl Country Club 41
Kahuku Golf Course 42
Ted Makalena Golf Course 42
Pali Golf Course 43
Olomana Golf Links 44
Honolulu International Country Club 45
Hawaii Country Club 45
Waikele Golf Club 46
Mililani Golf Club 48
Bayview Golf Center 49
Moanalua Golf Club 49
Waialae Country Club 49
West Loch Municipal Golf Course 51

Hawaii Kai Golf Courses 52

BIG ISLAND
Aloha Big Island 53
Kona Country Club & the Ali'i Golf Course 55
Waimea Golf Course 58
Hapuna Golf Course 61
Mauna Kea Golf Course 64
Makalei Hawaii Country Club 68
Waikoloa Golf Club 72
Discovery Harbor 74
Waikoloa Village Golf Course 75
Volcano Golf & Country Club 76
Sea Mountain at Punalu'u 77
Hilo Municipal Golf Course 77
Hamakua Country Club 78
Naniloa Country Club 79
Mauna Lani Resort (Francis H. I'i Brown Course) ... 80

KAUAI
Aloha Kauai 83
Princeville 86
Kiahuna Golf Club 89
Kauai Lagoons Golf & Racquet Club 90
Poipu Bay Resort Golf Course 93
Wailua Golf Course 96
Kukuiolono Golf Course 97

MOLOKAI
Kaluakoi Hotel & Golf Club 98
Ironwood Golf Course 98

LANAI
Aloha Lanai 99
The Experience at Koele 100
The Challenge at Manele 102
Quick Guide to Tee Time Reservations 104

ALOHA FROM THE ISLANDS

GOLF HAWAII was conceived as an informational resource to meet the demands of inquiring golfers worldwide. Numerous other publications inform visitors of Hawaii tourist attractions, but GOLF HAWAII is the only up-to-date comprehensive guide to Hawaiian golf—valuable to tourist and local golfers alike.

We would like to extend our thanks to all of Hawaii's golf professionals and to the Aloha Section of the PGA for their help and cooperation without which this Guide would not be possible. Also, I would like to thank our advertisers without whom it would be impossible to update our information and photographs each year.

This year's GOLF HAWAII shows more courses than ever before—16 new courses have come on-stream within the last two and a half years. These new courses represent some of the finest work of such notable designers as Dick Nugent, Jack Nicklaus, Robert Trent Jones, Jr., Ted Robinson, Arnold Palmer and Ed Seay, Nelson Wright and the Pete Dye team. Each presents a different challenge and greatly improves the choices available to both local and tourist golfers.

You'll find all the courses in GOLF HAWAII's island-by-island sections, which include maps and comparison charts for quick reference. The GOLF HAWAII "Quick Guide," listing information/tee time phone numbers for all Hawaii's courses is on page 104.

Mahalo & Aloha,

Paul Vogelsberger
Publisher
GOLF HAWAII

GOLF HAWAII

Publisher & Editor
Paul Vogelsberger

Assistants to the Editor
Lark Church
Frances Vogelsberger
Susan Yamamoto

Contributing Photographers
Ann Cecil (Cover Photo)
John Severson
Paul Vogelsberger

Contributors
Lark Church

Advertising Sales
Paul Vogelsberger
4614 Kilauea Avenue, Suite 528
Honolulu, HI 96816
(808) 733-2800 U.S.A.

Michael Roth
Roth Communications
(808) 545-4061 U.S.A.
Fax: (808) 545-4094 U.S.A.

Mailing address: 4614 Kilauea Avenue, Suite 528, Honolulu, HI 96816. GOLF HAWAII, The Complete Guide (English edition) is published annually. © 1994 by Printech Hawaii © 8th Edition © December 1994. All rights reserved. No part of this publication may be reproduced in any form or by any means without the prior written consent of the Publisher. U.S. subscriptions: U.S. $9.95 + $3.00 postage. Limited edition hard cover version U.S. $19.95 + $4.75 postage. Foreign subscriptions: U.S. $9.95 + relevant postage. GOLF HAWAII weighs approximately 20 oz. Advertising rates are available upon request. GOLF HAWAII, The Complete Guide's distribution is worldwide. GOLF HAWAII retains all reprint rights. GOLF HAWAII is also available in a Japanese edition, published quarterly. For information, contact GOLF HAWAII at 4614 Kilauea Avenue, Suite 528, Honolulu, HI 96816.

MAUI

Course	No. of holes	Yardage	Rating	Par	Golf Cart Mandatory?	Cart Fees	Club Rental	Pro Shop	Driving Range	Night Lights	Restaurant	Cocktails	Green Fees	Course type
Kaanapali Golf Course (South Course)	18	Ch: 6555 M: 6067 W: 5485	72.1 69.5 71.6	71 71 71	yes	included	yes	yes	yes	no	yes	yes	Resort $90 Public $100	R
(North Course)	18	Ch: 6994 M: 6136 W: 5417	74.0 69.0 70.0	71 71 72	yes	included	yes	yes	yes	no	yes	yes	Resort $90 Public $100	R
Kapalua Golf Club (Bay Course)	18	Ch: 6600 M: 6051 W: 5124	71.7 69.2 69.6	72 72 72	yes	included	yes	yes	yes	no	yes	yes	Resort $77 Public $110	R
(Village Course)	18	Ch: 6632 M: 6001 W: 5134	73.3 70.4 70.9	71 71 72	yes	included	yes	yes	no	no	yes	yes	Resort $77 Public $110	R
(Plantation Course)	18	Ch: 7263 M: 6547 W: 5627	75.2 71.9 73.2	73 73 75	yes	included	yes	yes	no	no	yes	yes	Resort $82 Public $120	R
Makena Golf Course (South Course)	18	Ch: 6986 M: 6599 W: 5503	72.5 70.6 71.1	72 72 72	yes	included	yes	yes	yes	no	yes	yes	Resort $70 Public $110	R
(North Course)	18	Ch: 6914 M: 6567 W: 5303	72.0 70.3 70.9	72 72 72	yes	included	yes	yes	yes	no	yes	yes	Resort $70 Public $110	R
Maui Country Club	9	M: 6549 W: 5984	70.2 72.5	37 37	no	included	yes	yes	no	no	no	no	Public $35 (Mon. only)	PR
Pukalani Country Club	18	Ch: 6945 M: 6494 W: 5574	72.8 70.6 71.1	72 72 74	yes	included	yes	yes	yes	yes	yes	yes	Public $60	PU
Sandalwood Golf Course	18	Ch: 6469 M: 6011 W: 5162	70.6 68.3 64.8	72 72 72	yes	included	yes	yes	yes	no	yes	yes	Resort $65 Public $75	PU
Silversword Golf Course	18	Ch: 6801 M: 6404 W: 5265	72.0 70.6 70.0	71 71 71	yes	included	yes	yes	yes	yes	yes	yes	Public $65	PU
Grand Waikapu Country Club	18	Ch: 7105 M: 6647 W: 5425	74.0 71.9 - - -	72 72 72	yes	included	yes	yes	yes	no	yes	yes	Resort $100 Public $200	PR
Waiehu Municipal Golf Course	18	M: 6330 W: 5511	69.8 70.6	72 71	no	$7.50	yes	yes	yes	no	yes	yes	Wkday $25 Wkend $30	M
Wailea Golf Club (Blue Course)	18	Ch: 6758 M: 6152 W: 5291	71.6 68.9 72.0	72 72 72	yes	included	yes	yes	yes	no	yes	yes	Resort $85 Public $125	R
(Gold Course)	18	Ch: 7070 M: 6152 W: 5442	73.0 69.0 71.0	72 72 72	yes	included	yes	yes	yes	no	yes	yes	Resort $90 Public $130	R
(Emerald Course)	18	Ch: 6825 M: TBD W: TBD	TBD TBD TBD	72 72 72	yes	included	yes	yes	yes	no	yes	yes	Resort $85 Public $125	R

R = RESORT   PR = PRIVATE
PU = PUBLIC   M = MUNICIPAL
ALL RATES SUBJECT TO CHANGE

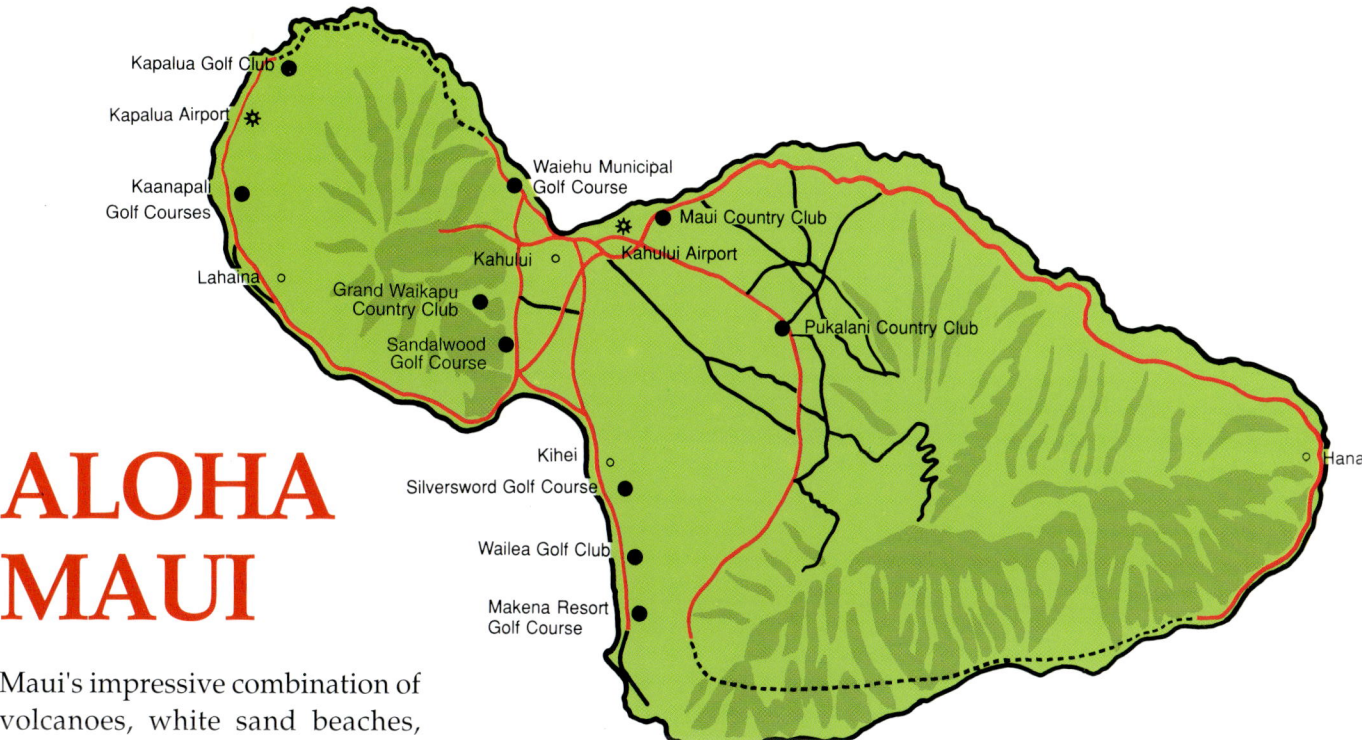

ALOHA MAUI

Maui's impressive combination of volcanoes, white sand beaches, lush tropical jungle and well-planned resort developments have helped make it the frequent choice of visitors.

It is, however, the quality of the courses (two private, one municipal, two public and nine championship/resort) that make Maui Hawaii's most popular island golfing destination.

On the west side of the island you can play the famous Kapalua Golf Course. Take your pick of two Arnold Palmer masterpieces -- the Village and Bay courses -- or the Coore and Crenshaw designed Plantation course. These courses offer a complete golfing experience and are a must for the visitor.

At the eastern end of Maui's south coast are the Wailea and Makena Golf Courses, two first-rate facilities with spectacular mountain and ocean views. Makena's new eighteen, the North Course, should prove to be a real challenge.

Wailea has just opened a new eighteen, the Emerald Course, which replaces the Orange Course.

Maui's newest resort complex includes two fine golf courses: Sandalwood Golf Course and the Grand Waikapu Country Club. Sandalwood is quickly becoming a favorite for local golfers, and can be a test of your skills regardless of how many rounds you play!

Maui no ka oi is a slogan you will hear often from proud Maui residents. It means "Maui is the best," a statement confirmed by the superior quality of its golf courses!

GOLF HAWAII
Presents

Hawaii's Greatest Golf Courses in a Spectacular Calendar!

From the islands of Oahu, Maui, Hawaii, Kauai and Lanai, GOLF HAWAII presents 12 of the most beautiful golf courses in the world in a colorful 10 ½" x 12" calendar. Order your 1995 calendar today for only $8.95 plus postage and handling. For P&H, U.S. add $2.90; Japan add $6.00. Send check or money order to: Printech Hawaii
4614 Kilauea Avenue, Suite 528
Honolulu, HI 96816 U.S.A.

Or order by Visa or Mastercard by mailing in your card number and expiration date to the above address or call U.S.A. (808) 733-2800. Please specify card.

Special bulk rates available for corporate orders with gold embossing & logo.

KAPALUA GOLF CLUB

The 11th hole of the Plantation Course.

Photo: Severson

The Kapalua Golf Club is probably the best known of Hawaii's golf courses. Kapalua's eye-catching logo adorns many a golf bag as a symbol of the discriminating golfer. This worldwide reputation is no simple coincidence, but the result of many hours and dollars of promotion and expenditures.

Following the lead of the AT&T at Pebble Beach and the Hawaiian Open at Waialae Country Club, Kapalua Land Company Tournament Director, Mark Rolfing, decided a major tournament would do wonders for Kapalua. Known initially as the Kapalua Open, the tournament became the Kapalua International and subsequently the Lincoln-Mercury Kapalua International, with prize money of $1,000,000 and a nationwide T.V. audience. In 1988, Kapalua also attracted the million-dollar Kirin Cup.

Of course, promotional ability and expense are not all it takes to make great golf. The other ingredient is great courses: two finely designed 18-hole Arnold Palmer masterpieces, the Bay and Village Courses, and the Coore & Crenshaw Plantation Course.

Situated on the extreme western point of Maui, Kapalua experiences weather typical and unique to the Hawaiian Islands. Hawaii's trades blow strong and consistent from the N.E. quadrant. These trades wrap around the West Maui mountains, bringing rain and gusty winds to Kapalua. The rain is mainly in the evening but the wind is definitely a force to be reckoned with. Not all holes are affected equally: some have Cook Pine wind breaks, others are in gullys and valleys, others are on windy ridges. Course design has cleverly integrated wind into play, so each course presents a different challenge.

The Bay Course, home of the Lincoln-Mercury Kapalua International, was completed in 1975. At par 72, it is 6,051 yards from the regular tee and offers demanding resort play. With a few changes, it becomes a PGA championship course, challenging even to the seasoned professional. The fairways are lush and green, as befits a quality course, and the panoramic views, which include adjacent plantations and the Pacific Ocean, can be seen from almost every hole.

"The hole that gives visiting golfers the most challenge on the Bay Course is No. 5," says Gary Planos,

Kapalua's Director of Golf. We believe him. This hole is anything from 135 yards to 205 yards. The tee shot is across a small bay that can either be calm and crystal clear or a raging mass of surf and spray. Either way, it is a distraction that prevents you from hitting your best shot. This is a hole where golfer after golfer either

The fourth hole of the Bay Course

ends up pearl diving or ricocheting all over the rocks before the green. The prevailing wind blows from behind, left to right. Here, the wind can actually help you get to the hole but you must allow for the left to right direction.

Ladies get a big break on No. 5. The front tee is to the left of the bay, not in front of it. There is still raging surf, but it is definitely less intimidating when you do not have to go over it. Arnold Palmer not only designed the course but he also holds the course record.

The Village Course offers a spec-

A spectacular view of the seventh hole of the Village Course with the Pacific in the distance.

Photo: Severson

tacular alternative in style to the Bay Course. This championship course resembles a meticulously maintained mountain course. Momentarily, you are transported off Hawaii. One would expect to encounter deer, bear and other wildlife roaming through the pines and ridges of Kapalua. Built in 1980, the course is built straight uphill for 6 holes with wind going left to right, and 9 holes going down with wind right to left of the holes blowing laterally to the slope. The Village is a well-balanced course, a challenge to the resort golfer as well as the pro. Add in 360-degree panoramic views and you have a very memorable game of golf indeed.

The view from the 5th, 6th and 7th is truly inspiring, from Makaluapuna Point through Honokahua Bay to the famous surfing point of Honolua Bay.

The No. 6 hole is a par 4 where the fairway has been cut through a forest of Cook Pines. There are pineapples on the left, a sticky lie and a lake on the right. The wind blows right to left but does not affect your first 60 yards or so due to the protective pines. The entrance to the green is on the left, enticing you into the pineapples. If you shoot to the right, your second shot is over a lake onto the undulating green. From the tee looking down, it appears to be a fairly straightforward hole, but if you do not concentrate, you could be in very big trouble.

Hole No. 13 is a par 4 dogleg right with three sand traps waiting for your first shot. Your second shot is through a narrow opening of trees onto the green . . . a bogey for most. Generally, rely on the break being toward Molokai Channel. The greens are described as medium to fast.

At the Bay and Village Course clubhouses, two award-winning golf shops offer the finest equipment and a wide assortment of fashionable accessories.

Both clubhouses offer excellent dining facilities. At the Village Course, the Village Cafe is open from 6:30 a.m. to 7:00 p.m. daily. The Bay Course clubhouse features the popular Bar & Grill, which is open for lunch and dinner and specializes in seafood, lamb and pasta dishes.

To undergo the total experience of Kapalua is to discover why Golf Magazine testifies "the Kapalua courses are unquestionably the finest 36-hole layout in Hawaii," and has awarded Kapalua its prestigious gold medal for U.S. golf resorts.

KAPALUA PLANTATION COURSE

The Plantation Course, opened for play since May 1991, is also home of the renowned Lincoln-Mercury Kapalua International. Like the Village and Bay courses, Kapalua's third championship course blends perfectly with the environment, taking maximum advantage of the terrain's natural characteristics.

The dramatic vistas, sweeping slopes, native vegetation and deep valleys that served as the plantation's landscape for generations, has now taken on a new role. Designed by Coore & Crenshaw, Inc., the Plantation Course is a long 18 holes with a par of 73 and yardage of 7,263. With understated design, Coore & Crenshaw have developed a course which is challenging and enjoyable to players of all skill levels.

As Bill Coore explains it, "Golf at the Plantation Course is golf on a grand scale. The design features within the course are large because the land on which they were created is open, windswept and immense. We've made every effort to apply time-honored architectural principles to a site so naturally spectacular and so expansive as to be rarely found in golf."

The Plantation Course opening hole introduces the character, scale and drama of the course. It is a downhill, downwind par 4 of immense proportion. An adequate tee shot, assisted by the wind and slope, should leave a middle-to-long iron approach to an expansive and welcoming green that slopes from left to

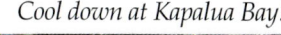
Cool down at Kapalua Bay!

right. The difficulty of this hole is more psychological than physical.

The 11th hole is the last par 3 of the course. At 164 yards, it demands thought and finesse. The desired tee shot is a short iron that either "cuts" and "holds" into the wind, which is blowing from the player's right shoulder or one that allows for a drift and uses the approach and slope of the green for assistance. A shot flown directly to the back left pin will not likely be tried more than once.

The most difficult par 4 on the course is the thirteenth, a long 407 yards, made far longer and more difficult by wind. Low, boring tee shots and long iron or fairway wood approaches are necessary to reach this deep and deceptive green in regulation. Putts numbering three or more will also be commonplace, given the size, slope and the wind's effects.

In an age of "over grooming," it is interesting to note that the Plantation is in some respects a low maintenance course. The grass is allowed to grow over the edge of bunkers and deep rough starts at the very edge of fairways. This approach is refreshing and the visual impact can transport you back to another time and place of traditional golf course layout. Greens and fairways, however, show signs of high maintenance and excellent greenskeeping.

The Plantation Clubhouse is an elegant structure of 33,000 square feet, offering the finest in amenities, including dining facilities, a well-stocked golf shop and a large locker room.

Director of Golf:
Gary Planos

For further information:
Kapalua Golf Club
300 Kapalua Drive
Kapalua, Maui, HI 96761
(808) 669-8044

From the first hole, the scale and drama of the Plantation unfolds.

Photo: Severson

Kaanapali Golf Courses

In the heart of Maui's premiere resort complex are the Kaanapali Golf Courses, 36 holes of perfect resort golf. The fairways and greens are well kept, despite over 100,000 rounds played each year.

The **North Course** was built in 1961, another masterstroke of Robert Trent Jones, Sr. Designed primarily for resort play, the North Course has sufficient challenge and character for major tournaments, like the World Cup, the LPGA Kemper Open (for four years) and the GTE Kaanapali Classic PGA Senior's Tour.

At par 71, the North Course is 6,136 yards from the men's tee. The emphasis is on putting: greens are large and contoured to the mountainous terrain, deliberately kept slow except during tournaments.

Director of Golf Ray DeMello considers the 14th and 18th holes the most challenging. The 14th hole is a long par 4 dogleg left. If the wind is behind you, you will use only short clubs. Four bunkers await your tee shot, three protecting the green. Next to the green, bikini-clad bathers promenade along the beach -- an unexpected sand hazard.

The 18th is the next most challenging, a par 4 measuring 438 yards with water running the entire right side and wind blowing over your shoulder from left to right.

"The 18th gives you a choice," says DeMello. "Go over the water to a green 60 feet wide, or play the green straight where it is, 20 feet wide with a bunker on one side and a lake on the other." DeMello advises, "Play your tee shot to the right of the fairway. You'll go over water on your second shot to a larger target... but think carefully about club selection."

The **South Course** came in response to the growth of Kaanapali Resort. Commissioned in 1970 to build a course offering leisurely play for high handicappers, Arthur

Play Kaanapali when you're ready to graduate to a Senior PGA TOUR course.

Now's your chance to play the very same courses the Seniors play year after year. Home of the Hyatt Regency Maui Kaanapali Classic, the only Senior PGA TOUR stop in Hawaii, Kaanapali Golf Courses offer breathtaking views of the ocean, West Maui mountains, and neighboring islands of Molokai and Lanai. So graduate to the courses where the best love to play – the courses of Kaanapali.

KAANAPALI GOLF COURSES • Kaanapali Resort • Lahaina, Maui, Hawaii 96761
For tournament (October 24-30, 1994) or vacation information,
call 1-800-245-9229. Fax (808) 661-0203.

Kaanapali Golf Courses

Jack Snyder was re-commissioned seven years later to transform it into a regulation championship course. The result is Hawaiian-style golf with all the trappings of hills, water and wind.

The South Course is par 71, 6,067 yards from the men's tee. It is slightly shorter than the North Course, with narrower fairways.

"You really have to pay attention on the South Course," says DeMello. "You lull yourself into a false sense of security. It looks wide open -- then boom! You're out of bounds or in a bunker."

An example is the 8th, a par 5, 537 yards, the toughest hole on the South Course, with sugar cane fields on both sides, the prevailing wind against you and a well-trapped, undulating green.

The sights from the Kaanapali Courses are amazing. Many holes afford mountain, ocean and island views. On the South Course 4th hole, a turn-of-the-century sugar cane train chugs by carrying visitors from Kaanapali Resort to Lahaina. Or try sinking a putt on the North Course 14th while watching jumping humpback whales out of the corner of your eye!

There is no time like the present to enjoy it all!

Director of Golf:
Ray DeMello

For further information:
Kaanapali Golf Courses
Kaanapali Resort
Lahaina, Maui, HI 96761
(808) 661-3691

The 4th hole of the North Course.

WAILEA GOLF CLUB

Wailea's Gold Course features lava rock and native Hawaiian grasses.

When they chose the site for the Wailea Golf Club, they really did their homework. Situated on the lee side of Maui's famous dormant volcano, Mt. Haleakala, Wailea receives only 11 inches of rain annually and is sheltered from the usual gusty Hawaiian tradewinds.

The Wailea golf complex includes three 18's: the Blue Course, the Gold Course and the brand new Emerald Course.

The Blue course, designed by Arthur Jack Snyder, opened in 1972 and its great views, brightly colored foliage -- hibiscus, plumeria and bougainvillea -- and somewhat forgiving fairways have made it a favorite with resort golfers ever since.

The Blue's 8th hole is a challenge, a 430-yard, par 4 with a fairway bunker and trees guarding the right side. Bunkers flank both sides of a fast, undulating green.

At 420 yards from the back tee, No. 13 is a long par 4. It is a sharp dogleg left with out-of-bounds on the left and the right. You have to hit the ball very straight. Aim left and you hit trees. Aim right and you have a big lava rock formation to contend with. The green is well-guarded by three bunkers.

Robert Trent Jones, Jr. is the creator of the Gold course. The Gold is a sharp departure from the Blue: no pretty flowers and fountains here, but rather a rugged, more classic golf course design featuring narrow fairways, ancient lava rock walls and gardens of native Hawaiian grasses. At 7,070 yards, the Gold is also a little longer than the Blue.

The Gold's par 5 seventh is a long, challenging hole, a double dogleg that climbs 580 yards uphill and into the wind.

Another tough hole is the par 3 eighth. While the card says 190 yards, the wind is at your back and you are on an elevated tee. Just how much wind is the key -- choose your club wisely!

The Emerald Course, opened in December 1994, replaces the old Orange Course. Jones also designed this par-72, 6,825-yard course which boasts of spectacular mountain and ocean views and lush landscaping.

Wailea has added a clubhouse to service the Gold and Emerald courses, and built a state-of-the-art practice facility. Like the Blue's clubhouse, the new clubhouse offers a full service pro shop, locker rooms, rentals and a delightful restaurant serving great sandwiches and very cold beer. Worth the stop!

Head Professional:
Rick Castillo

For further information:
Wailea Golf Club
120 Kaukahi Street
Wailea, Maui, HI 96753
(808) 879-2966

MAUI COUNTRY CLUB

Opening way back in 1927, Maui Country Club was the first golf course built on the island, and it is one of Maui's few private club facilities.

Architects Alex Bell and William McEwen designed this little gem of a course which is highly appreciated by local Mauians and the few fortunate visiting players.

The looks of this course are fairly straightforward. There is no water, no fairway bunkers, no doglegs, no hills and in most cases the greens are flat. But add to this a head-on wind averaging 20 mph during the summer months and the whole situation changes. It looks easy, but it is not.

Maui Country Club's nine holes are played on different tees in and out to provide 18 holes of 6,549 yards of golf with a par of 74. The fairways and grounds are dotted with coconut palms, ironwood and lush banyan trees.

The clubhouse and restaurant are in a cool plantation-style building that transports one back in time to a simpler Hawaii. Complete with tennis courts and swimming pool, Maui Country Club prides itself on being a club for the whole family.

Guests are welcome when accompanied by a member and outside visitors are allowed to play every Monday.

For further information:
Maui Country Club
48 Nonohe Place
Paia, Maui, HI 96779
(808) 877-0616

SILVERSWORD GOLF CLUB

Nestled in the valley between the West Maui Mountains and Mt. Haleakala, Silversword Golf Club is central to most of Maui's population centers and is particularly close to Kihei and the Wailea resort areas.

Expect dry, breezy conditions at Silversword. The Kihei area normally receives only about 3" of rain annually. In late afternoon the wind for which Maui is famous rushes down through the valley from the north in powerful gusts, so an early tee time makes for a much easier round.

Designed by course architect W. J. Newis and opened in 1987, Silversword has a balanced number of holes going into, away from and across the prevailing winds.

This 6,003 yards par 71 layout offers many challenges. The 440-yard 9th hole is a long par 4 into the trade winds with out-of-bounds on the left side. Water can come into play here and the green is two-tiered.

The 14th hole, a par 3 measuring 165 yards from the blue tee, has an elevated green that requires a high, accurate, soft shot.

All in all, Silversword is a fine golf course, still maturing but already providing exciting golf with spectacular views and wonderful sunsets.

Silversword Golf Club has a full-service pro shop and a lighted driving range. The Silversword Restaurant here is worth visiting. In addition to the customary fare, they serve a "French style Hawaiian plate lunch." Sound intriguing? Try it!

For further information:
Silversword Golf Club
1345 Piilani Highway
Kihei, Maui, HI 96753
(808) 874-0777

15

MAKENA GOLF COURSE

The South Course's 16th hole offers an excellent view of the sparkling blue waters of the Pacific.

Makena Golf Course brings to mind the old cliche: "The best kept secret in town." Here you'll find one of the better quality, if less well-known, resort courses in Hawaii.

Like its neighbor, Wailea Golf Course, Makena has the best weather imaginable for golf. Protected by the dormant Haleakala volcano, Makena is blessed with 80-degree, rainless days and is spared the strong tradewinds that pervade much of Maui. When the weather turns hot, a cloud cover forms over Haleakala bringing welcome relief from the scorching sun.

Makena Golf Course has been redesigned in recent years and is now two eighteens, the South and the North Courses. Design of the original Makena as well as the two new courses is by master resort golf architect Robert Trent Jones, Jr.

Both courses feature Jones' trademark rolling fairways, multiple hazards and undulating greens, and both offer a bevy of breathtaking views.

Jones redesigned the 6,599-yard, par 72 South Course by creating a new front nine for the original Makena course. The South is said to be the more forgiving of the new Makena lineup, particularly on the fairways. However, no one can truthfully call this eighteen a pushover!

The South 15th is a magnificent 183-yard par 3 ocean hole with a downhill tee shot. Beyond the green are palm trees, the Pacific and in the distance, the island of Kahoolawe

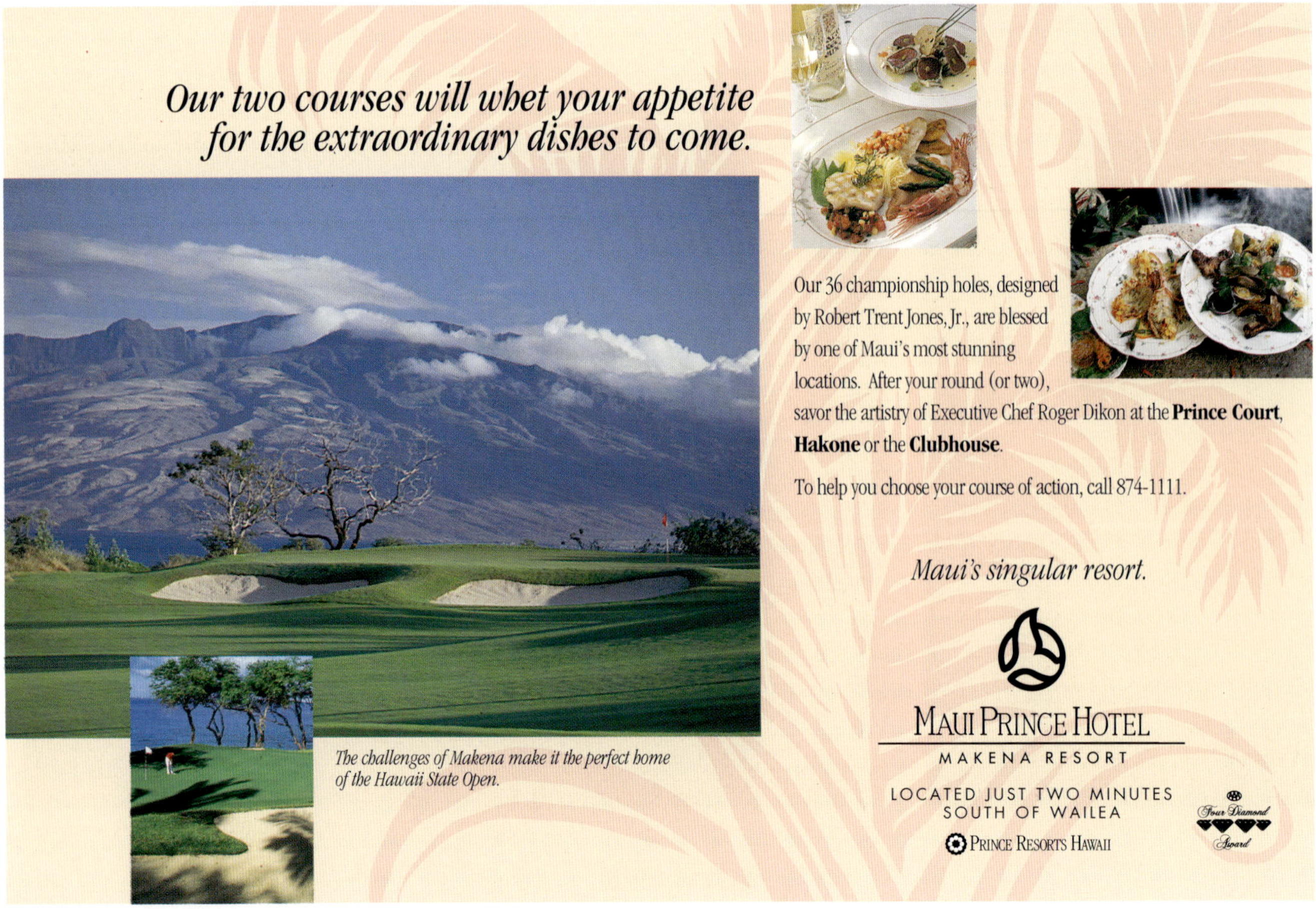

Our two courses will whet your appetite for the extraordinary dishes to come.

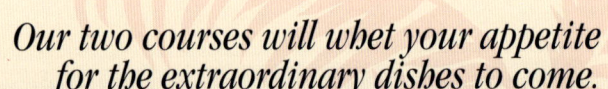

Our 36 championship holes, designed by Robert Trent Jones, Jr., are blessed by one of Maui's most stunning locations. After your round (or two), savor the artistry of Executive Chef Roger Dikon at the **Prince Court**, **Hakone** or the **Clubhouse**.

To help you choose your course of action, call 874-1111.

Maui's singular resort.

The challenges of Makena make it the perfect home of the Hawaii State Open.

Maui Prince Hotel
MAKENA RESORT

LOCATED JUST TWO MINUTES
SOUTH OF WAILEA

The South 15th -- a beautiful par 3.

and the crescent rim of the sunken volcano of Molokini. The view is a distraction, but so is the deep sand trap fronting most of the green. Should you overshoot, you could wind up in the ocean.

The South's next hole, the 385-yard 16th, is a par 4 paralleling the beach. Palm trees and ironwoods border the fairways. There is a radical break towards the beach and that is where a lot of golfers lie after their first shot, particularly when the winds are up. The flag is not visible for your second stroke and twin bunkers flank the two-tiered green, with a third behind. Once you are on the green, the hole is still only half-over. Its quick undulating surface has drawn many a bogey from players expecting a par.

The par 72 North Course, which opened at the end of 1993, is 7,000 yards of challenging golf, with narrow fairways, tight doglegs and, in particular, tough-to-read greens. This is one of those courses that only becomes reasonable once you have played it a time or two and gotten the feel of the greens. As a general rule, play the greens defensively by staying below the pin on your approach -- give yourself a pat on the back when you two-putt.

A good example is the North 16th, which is actually an update of the original Makena 7th hole. A 390-yard par 4, it doglegs sharply left. Even if you can cut the dogleg, your approach shot is an awkward angle onto a pencil-thin green. And once on, reading multiple breaks on an undulating green is just plain hard to do. Best strategy: pray for par!

Whether you are a visitor to Maui or a resident, be sure to put Makena Golf Course in your golfing plans. The new North course alone is worth the trip. Here, at less cost than its sister courses, you'll experience resort championship-style golf at its best.

Director of Golf
Howard Kihune, Jr.

For further information:
Makena Golf Course
5415 Makena Alanui
Kihei, Maui, HI 96753.
(808) 879-3344

PUKALANI COUNTRY CLUB

Located 1,500 feet up the slopes of Maui's famous Mount Haleakala, Pukalani Country Club is a blessing for golfers who appreciate a well-kept course at a reasonable price.

Designed by course architect Bob Baldock, Pukalani has a hilly layout, with undulating fairways protected by majestic Italian cypress pines. Greens are slow to medium but the breaks are definitely there, so keep concentrating.

The 3rd hole at Pukalani is the most interesting, a 136-yard par 3 offering a choice of two greens.

Shoot over a gaping gully filled with kiawe and eucalyptus trees to a green that looks very far away, or shoot over a 60-foot cliff onto a green guarded by palm trees. Most players go over the cliff.

Pukalani's restaurant is definitely worth a try. The eclectic menu includes traditional Hawaiian fare, without the fanfare of standard resort luaus.

Other course facilities include a pro shop and a lighted driving range, open to 9 p.m.

For further information:
Pukalani Country Club
360 Pukalani Street
Pukalani, Maui, HI 96788
(808) 572-1314

Sandalwood Golf Course & Grand Waikapu Country Club

The Waikapu resort complex includes two golf courses: Sandalwood Golf Course, open for public play; and Grand Waikapu Country Club, originally a private club limited to membership play, now also open for public play.

Nestled among the keawe trees on the southern end of the Waikapu resort complex is the Sandalwood Golf Course. At 6,469 yards from the blue tees, the Nelson Wright group of architects has designed a pleasantly challenging course which is quickly becoming a favorite for Maui's local golfers.

Sandalwood can be a test regardless of how many rounds you play. The course contains three large water hazards as well as a generous application of well-shaped bunkers. The famous Maui winds can also become your enemy: the use of an extra club or two will be essential in typical 15-20 mph tradewind gusts.

However, that same wind can become your ally, as on the #1 handicap hole, the 3rd, a par 5 measuring 549 yards. This signature hole plays downwind and the green is reachable in two if you can avoid the bunkers on the right, not to mention the lake which extends from 135 yards out all the way to almost the front edge of the green.

Sandalwood's par 3's are definitely championship caliber and a main feature of the course. When you step up to the elevated tee box that rises 60 feet above the 4th hole, it's a breathtaking moment: with the majestic view of Maalaea Harbor, it's difficult to concentrate on the imposing shot before you!

Like an inspired artist, noted golf course architect Ted Robinson has created a Bermuda masterpiece in the Grand Waikapu Country Club course. Like the stroke of a master artist's brush, Mr. Robinson has layered the slopes of the West Maui Mountains with a texture of 7,105 championship yards of undulating greens and fairways. Holes 11 and 18 -- both par 5's -- are Robinson's two favorites, with intimidating bunkers on the 14th and a dominant water hazard on the 18th.

Head Professional
Fran Cipro

For further information:
Sandalwood Golf Course
Grand Waikapu Country Club
2500 Honoapiilani Highway
Wailuku, Maui, HI 96793
(808) 242-4653 (Sandalwood)
(808) 244-7888 (Grand Waikapu)

WAIEHU MUNICIPAL GOLF COURSE

Rarely do you fall in love with a municipal course. But rarely does one encounter a municipal course running alongside palm fringed sandy beaches. Here on Maui's north shore, Waiehu Municipal Golf Course does exactly that.

The first nine was built way back in 1928. The second was completed in 1966. Being the least expensive course on Maui, Waiehu sees plenty of play. Locals line up early to take advantage of this rare bargain. And, of course, the fairways suffer. Not always as green or as well kept as its southern neighbors in the tournament belt, Waiehu is still a course that is a challenge and fun to play.

On the second hole, you shoot over a pond to a well protected green and on the fifth, a par 3, the tee shot is from a well elevated tee that makes the green look closer than it really is. The northeast trade winds really complicate the game for those who are not used to it. But local players know it well, as the north shore of Maui has the most consistent and strong trade winds of all the Hawaiian Islands.

Director of Golf:
Art Rego

For further information:
Waiehu Municipal Golf Course
P.O. Box 507
Waiehu, Maui, HI 96753
(808) 243-7400

OAHU

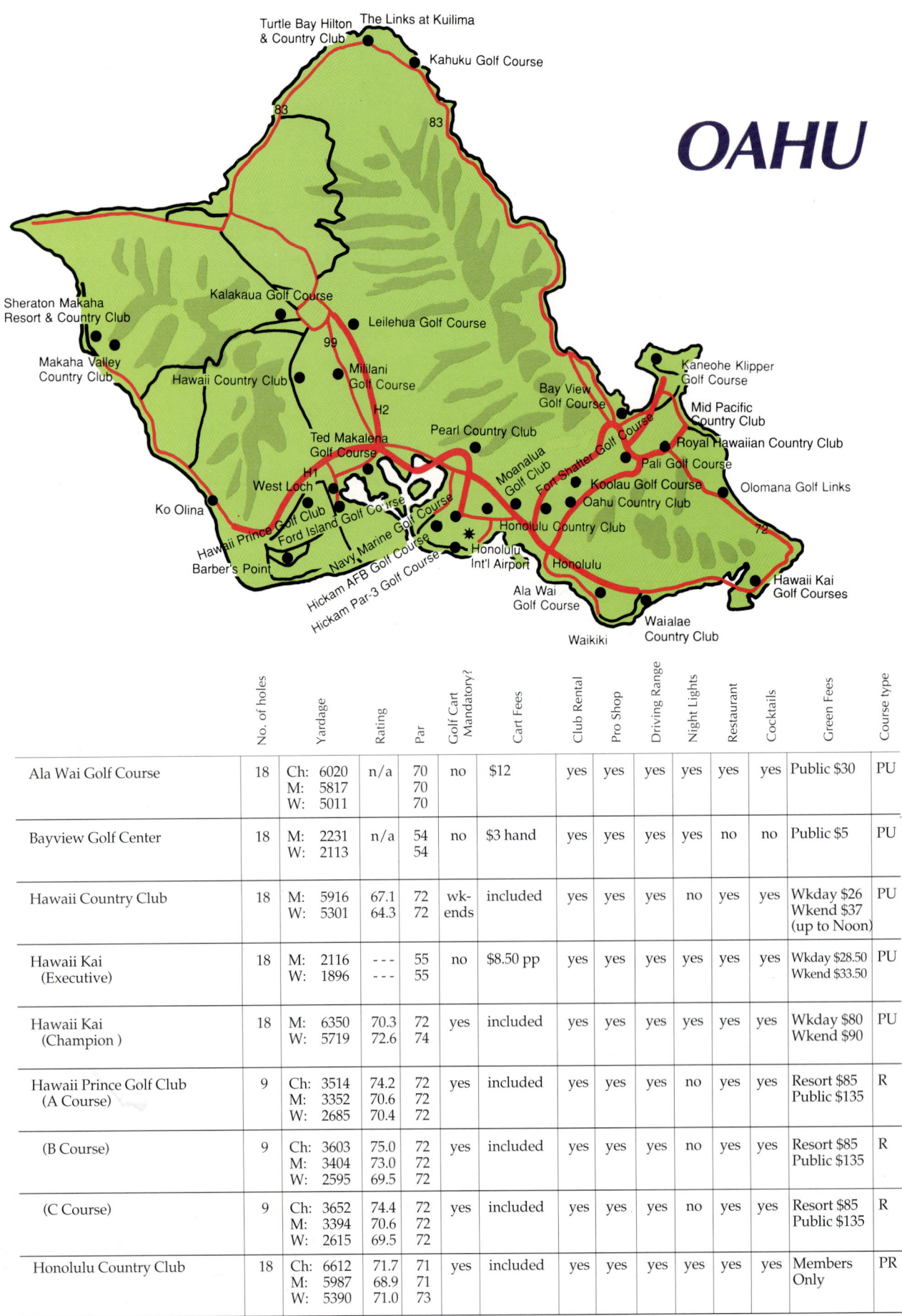

	No. of holes	Yardage	Rating	Par	Golf Cart Mandatory?	Cart Fees	Club Rental	Pro Shop	Driving Range	Night Lights	Restaurant	Cocktails	Green Fees	Course type
Ala Wai Golf Course	18	Ch: 6020 M: 5817 W: 5011	n/a	70 70 70	no	$12	yes	yes	yes	yes	yes	yes	Public $30	PU
Bayview Golf Center	18	M: 2231 W: 2113	n/a	54 54	no	$3 hand	yes	yes	yes	yes	no	no	Public $5	PU
Hawaii Country Club	18	M: 5916 W: 5301	67.1 64.3	72 72	wk-ends	included	yes	yes	yes	no	yes	yes	Wkday $26 Wkend $37 (up to Noon)	PU
Hawaii Kai (Executive)	18	M: 2116 W: 1896	--- ---	55 55	no	$8.50 pp	yes	yes	yes	yes	yes	yes	Wkday $28.50 Wkend $33.50	PU
Hawaii Kai (Champion)	18	M: 6350 W: 5719	70.3 72.6	72 74	yes	included	yes	yes	yes	yes	yes	yes	Wkday $80 Wkend $90	PU
Hawaii Prince Golf Club (A Course)	9	Ch: 3514 M: 3352 W: 2685	74.2 70.6 70.4	72 72 72	yes	included	yes	yes	yes	no	yes	yes	Resort $85 Public $135	R
(B Course)	9	Ch: 3603 M: 3404 W: 2595	75.0 73.0 69.5	72 72 72	yes	included	yes	yes	yes	no	yes	yes	Resort $85 Public $135	R
(C Course)	9	Ch: 3652 M: 3394 W: 2615	74.4 70.6 69.5	72 72 72	yes	included	yes	yes	yes	no	yes	yes	Resort $85 Public $135	R
Honolulu Country Club	18	Ch: 6612 M: 5987 W: 5390	71.7 68.9 71.0	71 71 73	yes	included	yes	yes	yes	yes	yes	yes	Members Only	PR

OAHU

R = RESORT PR = PRIVATE
PU = PUBLIC M = MUNICIPAL
ALL RATES SUBJECT TO CHANGE

Course	No. of holes	Yardage	Rating	Par	Golf Cart Mandatory?	Cart Fees	Club Rental	Pro Shop	Driving Range	Night Lights	Restaurant	Cocktails	Green Fees	Course type
Kahuku Golf Course	9	M: 2700 W: 2700	65.4 67.4	35 36	no	n/a	yes	no	yes	no	no	no	$19 $30 /2 rnds	PU
Ko Olina Resort	18	Ch: 6867 M: 6324 W: 5358	72.9 70.8 71.2	72 72 72	yes	included	yes	yes	yes	no	yes	yes	Resort $85 Public $130	PU
Koolau Golf Course	18	Ch: 7310 M: 6455 W: 5119	76.4 72.5 72.9	72 72 72	no	included	yes	yes	yes	no	yes	no	Resort $85 Public $100	PU
The Links at Kuilima	18	Ch: 7199 M: 6795 W: 5574	75.0 73.2 67.6	72 72 72	yes	included	yes	yes	yes	no	yes	yes	Resort $75 Public $99	R
Makaha Valley Country Club	18	Ch: 6369 M: 6091 W: 5720	69.2 67.6 72.7	71 71 71	yes	included	yes	yes	yes	no	yes	yes	Public $80	PU
Ted Makalena Golf Course	18	M: 5946 W: 5551	71.2 71.2	71 73	no	$12	yes	yes	no	no	yes	yes	Public $30	PU
Mid Pacific Country Club	18	Ch: 6784 M: 6461 W: 5991	73.2 71.6 77.9	72 72 72	yes	included	yes	yes	no	yes	yes	yes	Member's guest $50	PR
Mililani Golf Course	18	Ch: 6455 M: 6239 W: 5985	69.3 68.1 72.8	72 72 72	yes	included	yes	yes	yes	yes	yes	yes	Wkday $80 Wkend $88	PU
Moanalua Golf Club	9	M: 2972 W: 2939	67.8 72.9	72 72	no	$9	yes	yes	no	no	yes	yes	Wkday $20 Wkend $25	PR
Olomana Golf Links	18	Ch: 6326 M: 5887 W: 5561	70.3 68.2 73.3	72 72 73	yes	included	yes	yes	no	yes	yes	yes	Public $80	PU
Pali Golf Course	18	Ch: 6754 M: 6494 W: 6080	- - - 70.4 74.5	72 72 73	no	$12	yes	yes	no	yes	no	no	Public $30	PU
Pearl Country Club	18	Ch: 6750 M: 6230 W: 5489	72.5 69.5 70.2	72 72 72	yes	included	yes	yes	yes	yes	yes	yes	Wkday $70 Wkend $75	PU
Royal Hawaiian Golf Club	18	Ch: 6455 M: 6005 W: 4463	70.9 68.8 67.4	70 70 70	yes	included	yes	yes	yes	no	yes	yes	Member's Guest $60 Public $80	PR
Sheraton Makaha Resort & Country Club	18	Ch: 7091 M: 6414 W: 5880	73.2 70.6 73.9	72 72 72	yes	included	yes	yes	yes	no	yes	yes	Resort $80 Public $150 Resident $65	R
Turtle Bay Country Club	9	M: 6050 W: 5165	- - - - - -	70 70	yes	included	yes	yes	yes	no	yes	yes	Resort $50 Public $55	R
Waialae Country Club	18	Ch: 6906 M: 6529 W: 5753	73.2 71.7 72.4	72 72 72	yes	included	yes	yes	yes	no	yes	yes	Member's Guest $50	PR
West Loch Municipal Golf Course	18	Ch: 6479 M: 5849 W: 5296	70.3 67.8 68.6	72 72 72	yes	$6 pp	yes	yes	yes	yes	yes	yes	Public $30	M
Waikele Golf Club	18	Ch: 6663 M: 6261 W: 5226	71.7 69.9 69.3	72 72 72	yes	included	yes	yes	yes	no	yes	yes	Wkday $90 Wkend $95	PU

ALOHA OAHU

Oahu is the third largest and most populous island in the Hawaiian chain. Known to Hawaiians as the "Gathering Place," Oahu, with 34 courses, offers more golfing choices than its neighboring islands.

Over the past 3 years Oahu has seen the opening of five new golf courses. Each of these new clubs has something unique to offer.

On Oahu's North Shore next to Turtle Bay Country Club is the Links at Kuilima. This course winds through a wetland nature reserve and adjacent to the Pacific Ocean. According to designer Arnold Palmer, this course "is the closet to a Scottish Golf Links outside of Scotland."

On the leeward or "Ewa" side of the island, Waikele Golf Club typifies golf architect Ted Robinson's affinity for water, with ponds and waterfalls strategically placed throughout the course.

"Makai" of Waikele (i.e., towards the ocean) lies the Hawaii Prince Golf Club. Consisting of three 9-hole courses, the layout and design is to accomodate the various skills of Hawaii Prince Hotel guests.

By far the most exciting course to open is years is the breathtaking Koolau Golf Course. This course winds along the foot of the dramatic Koolau mountains, crossing jungle-covered ravines in the process. With a slope rating of 162 (the USGA maximum recognized slope is 155), this is the **toughest course** in the U.S.A. Course architect Dick Nugent has designed narrow fairways with ravines to cross over almost every hole. The greens are undulating and protected by lots of sand bunkers. Whew! Luckily the designer was intuitive enough to include a number of tee placements so that you can pick your level of challenge. If you are in Hawaii, this course is a must play.

The fifth course to open in recent years is located on the sunny western shore of Oahu at the Ko Olina Resort. This resort course is the cornerstone for the master-planned resort in which the Ihilani Resort and Spa has recently opened.

The Sheraton Mahaka Resort and Country Club, situated further west than the Ko Olina Resort, has been such a favorite for many years -- and still is.

Another course of note is the Ala Wai Golf Course, a municipal in the heart of Waikiki and reputed to be the busiest golf course in the world. The rates are right but the wait can be a bit bothersome. Another municipal which opened in the last three years is the West Loch Municipal. It also has reasonable green fees but due to extreme popularity it is wise to reserve a tee time well in advance.

Whatever your tastes, Oahu has a myriad of golf offerings from which to choose. We are sure you can find one to suit your location and level of play. Good luck!

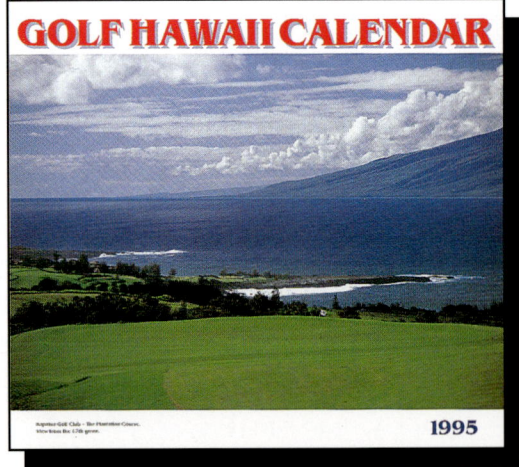

GOLF HAWAII
Presents

Hawaii's Greatest Golf Courses in a Spectacular Calendar!

From the islands of Oahu, Maui, Hawaii, Kauai and Lanai, GOLF HAWAII presents 12 of the most beautiful golf courses in the world in a colorful 10 ½" x 12" calendar.

Ideal for the home, office or as a special gift for the holiday season. Order your 1995 calendar of Hawaii's best golf courses today for only $8.95 plus postage and handling. For P&H, U.S. add $2.90; Japan add $6.00.

Send check or money order to:
Printech Hawaii
4614 Kilauea Avenue, Suite 528
Honolulu, HI 96816 U.S.A.

Or order by Visa or Mastercard by mailing in your card number and expiration date to the above address or call U.S.A. (808) 733-2800. Please specify card.

Special bulk rates available for corporate orders with gold embossing & logo.

Wind, water and sand add challenge to the Hawaii Prince's relatively flat fairways.

HAWAII PRINCE GOLF CLUB

Situated on the Ewa plain of Oahu's leeward coast some 30 minutes from downtown Honolulu, the 27 hole Hawaii Prince Golf Club is a necessary sporting attraction for guests of the Hawaii Prince Hotel and a welcome addition to the Hawaiian golfing scene.

The course is made up of three 9 holes, called the A, B and C courses. From the blue tees, the yardage is 3,352 on the A, 3,407 on the B and 3,394 on the C. Each is a par 36.

The Hawaii Prince is built on relatively flat land, so golf architects Ed Seay and Arnold Palmer have added plenty of water and sand to create a playable but strategically challenging golf layout.

For example, the 6th hole, a par 5, is 498 yards from the blue tee. Your best drive is a bit left of center of the fairway. The prevailing wind is a following wind moving left to right. Long hitters, beware: at 295 yards, there is a large sand trap in the middle of the fairway which you cannot see from the tee box. Others have to watch out for the first sand trap, waiting 220 yards out on the right side of the fairway. With strong trade winds, it is easy to end up here. Your shot has to stay left to avoid a large water hazard. You have to clear the two bunkers at 295 yards, and stay away from water on the right. The green is relatively small and slopes towards you with two bunkers at the back.

The 6th hole is typical of the Seay/Palmer course design. Careful study of the card and intelligent club choice are essential. If you land in a bunker -- and you will -- be sure to hit a good 2" behind the ball as the sand is very fine.

The Hawaii Prince clubhouse features all the characteristics of an upscale resort golf course, including a fully stocked pro shop with lots of logo wear, locker rooms and a restaurant and bar.

Director of Golf Operations:
Ted McAneeley

For further information:
Hawaii Prince Golf Club
91-1200 Fort Weaver Road
Ewa Beach, HI 96706
(808) 944-4567

The two-tiered green of Sheraton Makaha's 4th hole.

SHERATON MAKAHA RESORT AND COUNTRY CLUB

Forty minutes and a world away from the bright lights and crowds of Waikiki, golfers of all abilities from the world over are discovering the bold and exciting challenges of the Sheraton Makaha Resort and Country Club.

Nestled in a lush valley surrounded by the rugged cliffs of the Waianae Mountains, Sheraton Makaha Golf Course overlooks the golden sands of Makaha Beach and the blue Pacific, where each winter the world's best surfers compete.

On clear days, which means just about every day of the year at Sheraton Makaha, golfers can look out from virtually any tee or green on the course to see surfers riding the big waves, the wakes of fishing boats trolling or rain squalls moving across the ocean.

The valley was first settled by Polynesians in the 13th century. After the decline of Hawaii's feudal society, the valley knew a variety of owners. It once belonged to Governor Boki and his wife, Liliha. They ceded the valley to Chief Paki who eventually sold it to a group of Scottish and English ranchers, the Holt clan.

Cattle ranching, coffee and rice plantations were enterprises of the Holts. In the 1800's and 1900's, the valley was converted to sugar farming and ranching by the Waianae Plantation Company. You can still find remains of old plantation structures throughout the valley, reminders of Hawaii's unique early history.

In 1946, financier Chinn Ho successfully bid for the valley and began formulating his dream of creating a totally planned resort. In 1967, the West Course opened and two years later, the hotel was completed. In 1982, ITT Sheraton Corporation became the operators of the resort.

Sheraton Makaha Resort and Country Club offers an 18-hole championship course that was recently named by Golf Digest as one of the top 75 resort courses in the United States, the No. 1 golf course on Oahu and 6th in the state. Designed by William P. Bell, the course plays for 7,091 challenging yards from the championship tees and makes the most of nature's characteristics to create a course both aesthetically appealing and competitively invigorating. Panoramic vistas, sweeping slopes and native fauna

have all been left intact and incorporated within the course to provide a memorable golfing experience.

Rating for the course is 71.7 with 74.0 set for the championship course and 69.4 for the women's tees. The course slope rating of 140 is one of the highest in Hawaii. The par 72 course consists of four par threes, ten par fours and four par fives and features 69 sand bunkers and 10 water hazards.

The Sheraton Makaha golfing experience begins on a 550-yard par 5 from the championship tee with

a slight dogleg to the right. There is out-of-bounds to the left and large trees guarding the right side of the fairway. Proper placement of the drive from an elevated tee is critical as a large solitary tree sits right in the middle of the fairway about 187 yards from a green protected by large bunkers.

The most difficult hole is the 5th, a 460-yard par 4 with a tough dogleg right to a small, well-trapped green. The 14th hole, a 520-yard par 5, is another test of golf skills.

The last challenge on the course is the 370-yard 18th hole. It's not an especially long par 4 but the design of the hole makes it a fitting finale. Teeing off from a slightly elevated tee box, the golfer must take into consideration two fairway bunkers about 200 yards from the tee, out-of-bounds on the left, a lake on the right and another small pond guarding the approach to the green on the left front. Not to be forgotten are several good-sized trees behind the fairway bunkers which require some thought about club selection off the tee.

Also, around the 14th green on the back nine, don't be surprised to see peacocks near the green calmly appraising approach shots!

The secluded countryside offers the right environment for an exciting range of recreational activities in addition to golf. The resort offers day and night tennis, an Olympic-size pool and horseback riding into the scenic Makaha valley. Swimming, windsurfing, diving, sailing and fishing opportunites are just minutes away at world-famous Makaha Beach.

Head Professional:
Calvin Nelson

For further information:
Sheraton Makaha Resort
 & Country Club
84-626 Makaha Valley Road
Waianae, Oahu, HI 96792
(808) 695-9544

MID PACIFIC COUNTRY CLUB

A perfect day for golf reflects the perfect beauty of Mid Pacific.

For Oahu locals, there are no secrets about Lanikai. It is one of the most beautiful and desirable places to live on the whole island.

The ocean is alive at Lanikai. There is windsurfing, great fishing, snorkeling and the oldest of Hawaii sports, outrigger canoe paddling. It is a leisurely place with an abundance of sporting activities, among which is the exclusive and enjoyable Mid Pacific Country Club.

A mature course built in 1926, it offers 6,900 yards of challenges and is often favorably compared to Waialae. Originally carved out of kiawe forest by Alex Bell, the course now blends Norfolk pines and coconuts with the original kiawe.

The 8th hole is the one to remember. It is a 410-yard handicap-1 hole with a dogleg left, slightly uphill and against the wind. The way to play is to draw your ball along the tree line. Your second shot will need a four to five iron to the left. Hit the shot short of the hole so you have an uphill putt. Putting downhill is difficult since the greens are slick and quick.

The 15th hole is a dogleg right, 397 yards to an elevated green. You are hitting into a valley with an out-of-bounds right and trees left.

"What you have to do," says Mid Pacific Golf Pro, Mark Sousa, "is knock it straight down the middle. From there you have about a six iron shot left. Try to hit a slow punch shot into the wind. The greens will hold it down."

After the game, the Mid Pacific Country Club clubhouse is a great place to unwind. There is a swimming pool, sauna and a restaurant.

Head Professional:
Mark Sousa

For further information:
Mid Pacific Country Club
266 Kaelepulu Drive
Kailua, Oahu, HI 96734
(808) 261-9765

MAKAHA VALLEY COUNTRY CLUB

Makaha Valley Country Club is flanked by the Makaha-Keeau Ridge and the awe-inspiring Makaha Waianae Ridge -- a beautiful site for golf.

Designed by William Bell and finished in 1969, Makaha Valley is owned by Nitto Hawaii Co. Ltd., which also owns Maui's Silversword Golf Course. The course is a par 71, 6,091 yards from regular tees and 6,369 yards from championship.

Makaha Valley's third hole is one to remember, doglegging right with two water hazards awaiting your tee shot. It is best to pull up short and clear the water with your second shot. The green is protected by four bunkers.

The 4th hole is a 407-yard par 4 with a heavy break left and trees to the right. The fairway has gullies and ridges and the green is elevated but unprotected. This hole deserves its number one handicap.

Makaha is on the lee side of Oahu, so rain is not a problem. Winds are rarely more than a cooling 15 mph. Those fortunate enough to play Makaha will experience a beautiful course in perfect climate.

Makaha Valley has a full service pro shop and a restaurant. Scott Simpson is PGA touring pro. He is an inspiration to those who golf at Makaha.

For further information:
Makaha Valley Country Club
84-627 Makaha Valley Road
Waianae, Oahu, HI 96792
(808) 695-9578

KOOLAU GOLF COURSE

America's Toughest — Rated 155!

It is a fitting background for America's toughest golf course. A vista of pure drama, towering volcanic cliffs, dancing rainbows, waterfalls and the site of a historic masacre of thousands of Hawaiians by the great King Kamehameha. Nestled in the foothills of the windward side of Oahu's Koolau Mountains and only 35 minutes from Waikiki is the soon to be very famous Koolau Golf Course.

This Dick Nugent-designed course was rated over the official maximum slope rating by the USGA. The original rating for each tee was: gold 162, blue 158 and white 154. The rating was then reduced to comply with the USGA maximum of 155. In plain talk, be ready for the challenge and if you're not, then tee up from the silver or red course and enjoy the overall experience. With the longest yardage at 7310 from the gold and 5119 yards from the red, the difference can mean a lot to your final score.

The 1st hole sets the tone. A slight dog leg left par 5 that demands accuracy and distance off the tee. The fairway narrows and slopes right to left with bunkers on the right. Your second shot probably won't make the green, but set up your approach to clear the five bunkers that guard this undulating green. A par on this handicap 13 hole is an excellent start. Birdies will be few and far between.

The 2nd hole looks straight forward enough—382 yards from the blue tee with a very slight dog leg left. However, your drive should be to the right side of the fairway to have a good shot at a narrow undulating green. There are three bunkers guarding the green and they are very deep.

Ravines come into play and must be cleared on the 4th hole and again on the 5th, 6th, 7th, 8th, 10th, 11th, 12th, 13th, 14th, 16th and 18th. One could say Dick Nugent loves ravines!

On the 5th hole you have a choice of fairways. Across the ravine for a short iron to the green or to the left for a safer but longer shot that must also miss three bunkers on the left hand side of the green.

The back nine starts with a tough par 4. Another jungle-filled ravine lies downhill only 240 yards from the white tee. You have to lay up as close to the ravine as possible and with the downhill roll it's not easy. Take note also that the ravine is closer to the tee on the left hand side by an extra 40 yards. Your second shot must carry the ravine downhill to a well-bunkered green.

By the time you arrive at the 11th green, the view of Kaneohe

Oahu's majestic Koolau Mountains form a dramatic backdrop to the challenging 18th hole.

Bay in the distance may add some pleasure to what, for some, would be by now a humbling experience. Keep in mind that there are five tee placements to choose from and only single-digit handicap golfers should attempt to play from blue or gold tees.

By the 17th hole, nobody will have to convince you that Koolau Golf Course is America's toughest, but nothing prepares you for the 18th. This is the finishing hole of all times. At 432 yards from the white tee, this is their signature hole and handicap 1. A wide ravine separates the tee boxes from the fairway. You must carry about 200 yards to safety. For most players, their second shot will place them in a position to clear a very long bunker to a small green surrounded by more sand bunkers. Good luck!

The best thing about Koolau is

that you don't expect to reach a low score. You are there for the full experience of playing in the U.S.A.'s most difficult golf course and if you low score then it just makes the experience that much better.

The lavish Koolau Golf Course club house is still in the process of being built. The facilities for private functions are expected to be open before the end of 1995. In the temporary facility, there are snack and pro shops. The grounds are well maintained and the bent grass greens are a rare pleasure in Hawaii.

Koolau Golf Course is only 25 minutes from Honolulu, but can be a bit tricky to find since local government ordinances do not allow the golf course to place any signage on the turn off from the highway.

From Honolulu, take the Pali Highway across the Pali towards Kaneohe Bay. At the first turnoff as you drive down the Koolau Mountains, turn towards Kaneohe on Kamehameha Highway (Route #83). At about ½ mile there is a dip in the road. Approximately 300 yards away is a turnoff left onto Kionaole Road. Follow this winding road about ¾ mile to the club house entrance on your right.

If you are a visitor, ask your hotel about the Koolau Golf Course complementary pick-up.

Head Professional:
Parris Ernst

For further information:
Koolau Golf Course
45-550 Kionaole Road
Kaneohe, Oahu, HI 96744
(808) 236-4653

TAKE THE KOOLAU CHALLENGE!

"There are many things you can say about the Koolau Golf Course, but one thing is for sure . . . . It is the **TOUGHEST GOLF COURSE IN THE WHOLE U.S.A.**[*] . . . and that's official!"

—Parris Ernst, PGA Golf Pro

Unofficially, Koolau Golf Course is a masterpiece of the elements. Dick Nugent's design, the jungle-filled ravines, the towering cliffs, dancing rainbows, plunging waterfalls and spectacular views of Kaneohe Bay all go to make up the total experience that is the Koolau Golf Course.

Bring your best swing—and your camera!

KOOLAU GOLF COURSE
45-550 Kionaole Road • Kaneohe, Hawaii • 96744
For more information and tee times call **(808) 236-4653.**

*As rated by the USGA slope rating.

ROYAL HAWAIIAN COUNTRY CLUB

The Pete Dye team's design at Royal Hawaiian uses natural terrain to best advantage.

The Royal Hawaiian Country Club is located right off the busy Pali Highway that leads from Honolulu to Kailua. This beautiful new eighteen is a world unto itself, set in a deep valley ringed by the mighty Koolau Mountains.

Relatively short at 6,010 yards from the championship tees, this par 70 course is designed by the Pete Dye team and reflects his emphasis on making each hole an individual experience. From hole to hole you journey from wide open spaces on hillsides where wind is a factor to deep, dense jungle where an errant ball is lost forever.

At present, this course is two nines of an intended 36 holes. The King Kamehameha nine is a links-style par 35 and the Queen Liliuokalani nine is a traditional layout par 35. Course owners anticipate it will be a year or more until the two courses are completed. The current combination of two different course styles, added to the individuality of each hole's challenge, makes for a stimulating round.

The King's par 4 first hole measures 395 yards from the blue tee. The tee is elevated and provides a panoramic view of the course and surrounding volcanic mountains. The drive from the tee must take into account a banana tree-filled gully on the left cutting deep into mid-fairway and a large crystal-white bunker on the right. A good drive will lay-up to the right of the gully for a mid-iron approach shot. The fairway narrows as it approaches the green.

On both front and back nines, a design of narrow fairways, multiple hazards and sharp doglegs favors astute club selection and precision shot placement. Misjudge and your ball is gone -- roughs are truly rough here. Greens are often multi-tiered, ringed by hills, pocket bunkers and sharp dropoffs in the rear. Bermuda-grass greens run medium fast and generally break toward the ocean -- if you can figure out where the ocean is while putting in the jungle!

The back nine Queen course is a Hawaiian showcase of using natural terrain to best advantage. Many of the greens remain blind until the last moment.

The 14th hole is a 440-yard par 5 which doglegs left. The trees at the elbow of the dogleg are immense and the fairway is hemmed in on both sides by thick jungle. The target area for a drive has a long bunker on the left and a pocket bunker in the middle. The green is nowhere in sight. Safe play dictates a three wood layup at the elbow of the dogleg, and a second layup just short of a deep ravine 90 yards out from the pin. A big hitter may be able to reach the green in two by cutting the corner of the dogleg on the drive and gaining additional yardage as the ball rolls down a sloping fairway. However, the elevated green is long and narrow and has bunkers left and right. Good luck on a birdie attempt!

The Royal Hawaiian Country Club clubhouse, pro shop and restaurant are spacious and quietly elegant. Check out the view from the Japanese "furo" baths in the locker room -- it's not to be missed.

General Manager:
 Alan Hirata

For further information:
Royal Hawaiian Country Club
770 Auloa Road
Kailua, Oahu, HI 96734
(808) 262-2139

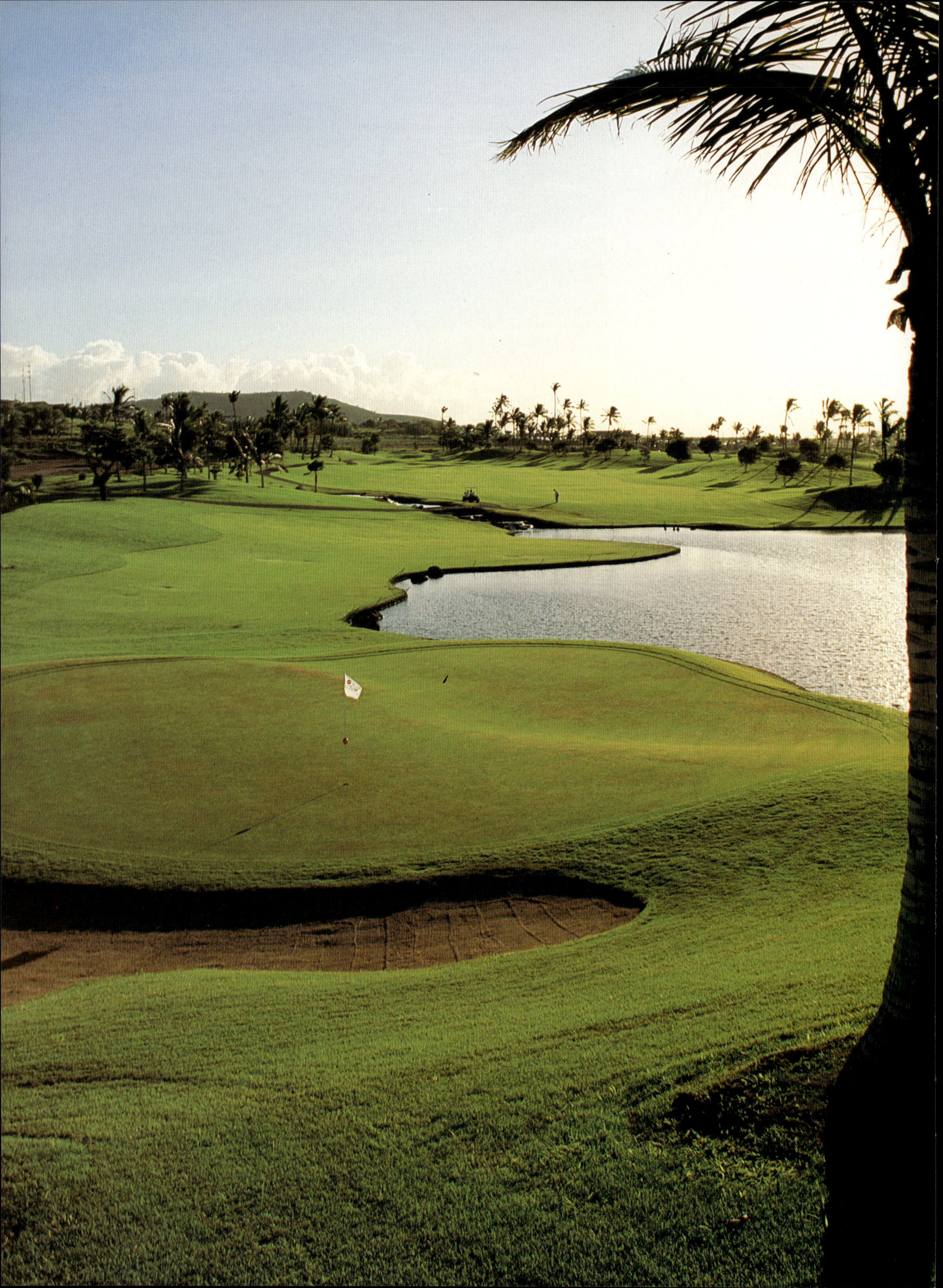

Precision shooting is required to reach Ko Olina's two-tiered, well-guarded 18th green.

KO OLINA GOLF CLUB & RESORT

Since its debut February 1, 1990, the distinctive Ko Olina Golf Club has developed a loyal coterie of golfers locally, nationally and internationally. Ko Olina was named America's Second Best New Course opened in 1990 by <u>Golf Digest</u>, and in 1992 was named one of "America's Top 75 Resort Courses" by the same publication.

As the cornerstone for the master-planned Ko Olina Resort, the golf club spared no expense in creating a golf experience that ranks among the finest in the islands. With an intriguing layout designed by Ted Robinson, the course itself is an array of Robinson's signature water features -- meandering streams, crashing falls and double-tiered lakes each flowing into another -- 16 spectacular water hazards in all. You are constantly serenaded with the sounds of rushing water. Some don't come into play for the average golfer but exist solely to provide a pleasant backdrop to the game.

The Ko Olina Golf Club is an exciting golf challenge that makes its way across 6,867 yards of the Ewa coastal plain. Robinson has moved over 2.5 million cubic yards of earth to put loads of movement and undulation into the course. He kept a close eye on the brisk trade winds that blow down the Ko'olau mountain range from the east.

Lining the par 72 course are hundreds of coconut palm trees, banyans, monkeypods and silver buttonwood trees, as well as flowering bougainvillaea, firecracker plants and fragrant plumeria. Tees and greens are planted with Tifton 328 and the fairways are lush with common bermuda.

The first of three signature holes on the course is the 537-yard 5th hole, a par 5. With lakes on the right side of the fairway immediately off the tee and a fairway bunker on the left fronting an elevated green, placement of the first two shots is critical. Even getting to the green is no guarantee of success, because it has a severe, two-tiered configuration that can easily result in three or more putts.

The sights and sounds of cascading water are everywhere on Ko Olina's final signature hole, the spectacular 429-yard 18th. A par 4, the 18th begins with seven pools on the right. A large lake and waterfall guard the left side of the elevated green. You have no choice but to play to the left, and approach the green over the last water feature. Says Robinson, "The drive on this hole is critical . . . A tournament can be easily decided on this final hole." An outdoor bar area, cantilevered over the lake, allows for outstanding viewing of your magnificent final approach shot into the sloping green!

As head professional at the Ko Olina Golf Club, Brad Weaver has been with the club since it opened in October, 1989. He supervises the crack team of golf professionals who provide lessons, supervise tee times and provide a full line of golf equipment and accessories. An enormous practice range lies adjacent to the clubhouse, with areas for lessons and golf schools and plenty of room for driving balls and practicing chips. Proper golf attire is required for all players: shirts with a collar are required for men.

Greens fees include cart rentals, complimentary bag tags, tees and ball markers. Twilight and early morning rates are available.

Ko Olina Golf Club has been the site of the ITOKI Hawaiian Ladies Open, an LPGA event featuring the best women professionals in the world. In addition, Ko Olina is represented both on the LPGA and PGA tours: Kris Tschetter is the touring professional on the LPGA circuit and Robert Gamez represents Ko Olina on a worldwide PGA tour basis.

Head Professional:
Brad Weaver

For further information:
Ko Olina Golf Club
92-1220 Aliinui Drive
Ewa Beach, Oahu, HI 96707
(808) 676-5300

ALA WAI GOLF COURSE

The busiest golf course on earth according to the Guinness Book of World Records is Hawaii's own, Ala Wai Municipal Golf Course. Nearly 500 rounds a day and 180,000 rounds a year fill all daylight hours and play often continues into the evening.

Ala Wai is a public golf course and with the extreme amount of play it gets, it is not surprising that it has not always been in the best of condition. Yet its unique and convenient location on the outskirts of Waikiki makes it a popular local and tourist attraction.

Obtaining a tee time, as one might expect, is no easy task. It is advisable, if you plan to play in a group of more than two, to call in at least a week before you want to play. Single golfers and twosomes can avoid a tee time and sign up on a waiting list on the day they wish to play. This, however, means a real wait. Expect two to four hours of serious relaxation before playing. There is a restaurant and putting green to keep you occupied as well as a new driving range that was installed in 1989.

Ala Wai Golf Course was completed in 1931 and was run by the Territorial Fair Commission until 1959. Following the abolition of the Commission, the City and County of Honolulu was given the land and after much deliberation allowed the golf course to remain as a municipal course. The course, as it turns out, is an incredibly valuable piece of real estate. Conservative estimates value the land at about $100 per square foot which can be attributed to its desirable commercial location.

The site of several local tournaments, notably the Ted Makalena State Open and the Mayor's Cup, Ala Wai is credited with having some demanding holes. Most avid golfers feel that the par 3 third hole and the par 3 twelfth hole are very tough tests of skill. Both require long and accurate iron shots to have a chance at par or better.

The dramatic 18th hole, bordering the Ala Wai canal, is as challenging as a finishing hole gets. The fairway is narrow, the green is small and right in the middle trickles a stream that runs into the canal. One way to play this hole is to tee off with a long iron which will set up a medium iron shot to the well-bunkered green.

Ala Wai's conditions are well suited to the general public. The layout is devoid of trees and thick grass. The wind, however, does play a role in club selection because of the wide-open terrain. "Mauka" or mountain showers occur almost daily but fortunately the rain is usually light and dissipates quickly.

Ala Wai Municipal underwent some major renovations of its front nine in 1989 when Nelson & Wright of Honolulu re-designed seven holes and added water. It would be called a water hazard but it does not come into play.

The rejuvenated Ala Wai now sports a $5 million club house that includes a restaurant, pro shop, lockers and a second floor community recreation hall. There is also a new driving range.

The new image does not figure to make the course any more popular than it already is - because it simply cannot be done!

Superintendent:
James Kawasaki

For further information:
Ala Wai Golf Course
404 Kapahulu Avenue
Honolulu, Oahu, HI 96815
(808) 296-4653

THE LINKS AT KUILIMA

The Links at Kuilima is the new sister course of Turtle Bay Country Club. Designed by the team of Ed Seay and Arnold Palmer, the par 72 course 6,225 yards from the men's tees, is ecologically sensitive: it surrounds a wetland preserve, Punahoolapa Marsh, which is home to endangered Hawaiian birds.

The course takes its name from the links design style and according to Palmer, "is the closest to a Scottish Golf Links outside of Scotland."

Multiple tee placement allows you to choose your level of play.

The front nine features sand, water, wind and rolling terrrain and is nearly devoid of trees and shrubs.

The back nine, by contrast, plays through a forest of ironwood pines and includes the course's signature 17th hole: 7 large bunkers run from the landing area to a green sitting just 100 feet from the ocean and Kahuku Point, the northernmost tip of Oahu.

Turtle Bay Country Club

Far from the maddening crowds of Waikiki, on Oahu's extreme northeast coast, the Turtle Bay Hilton and Country Club presents a perfect day's outing for the golfer.

The hotel was originally built by Del Webb with the intention of forming Hawaii's first gambling casino. Webb sold his share to Prudential, who hired the Hilton Corporation to manage the hotel and Arnold Palmer Golf Management to run the golf course.

Since then fairways and greens have been upgraded and the resort has blossomed as a whole. As Turtle Bay's ironwood trees have matured and its shrubbery grown in, wind has become less dominant as a factor.

Currently, the back nine is under renovation. Golfers play the front nine twice to reach their full 18 count.

Head Professional:
David Little

For further information:
Turtle Bay Golf & Tennis Resort
57-091 Kamehameha Highway
Kahuku, Oahu, HI 96731
(808) 293-8574

PEARL COUNTRY CLUB

Pearl is known for great golf and great views, like this one from the 11th green.

Pearl Country Club, located on the slopes of Aiea and overlooking Pearl Harbor, is well-known in Hawaii for many things. Among the most impressive are its convenient central location to Waikiki and to downtown Honolulu, its tree-lined rolling fairways and green valleys, and a panoramic view of the Pacific Ocean and the Waianae Mountain Range. Pearl is also the home course of David Ishii, the most successful Hawaii-born touring golf professsional and the winner of the 1990 United Hawaiian Open.

Designed by Akiro Sato, this picturesque 18-hole par 72 course follows the ebb and flow of Aiea's mountain slopes, maintaining the natural character of the landscape for challenging yet scenic play. Of the privately-owned courses open to the public on the island of Oahu, the Pearl Country Club is said to be the most popular among both local and tourist golfers.

At 6,230 yards from the men's tees, the course sometimes plays longer, especially when hitting into tricky tradewinds. Pearl is a course where club selection and accuracy take precedence over distance.

The new Pearl clubhouse opened in 1992 and features a 170-seat restaurant, banquet facilities for parties up to 300, an enlarged pro shop, lockers and showers. The lighted driving range is open six nights a week.

The Pearl Country Club offers the best of two worlds -- scenic and challenging golf, with easy accessibility to the exciting sights and sounds of Honolulu and Waikiki.

Head Professional:
Walter Kawakami

For further information:
Pearl Country Club
98-535 Kaonohi St
Aiea, Oahu, HI 96701
(808) 487-3802

KAHUKU GOLF COURSE

Looking for a departure from the norm? Too much refinement got you down? Try Kahuku Municipal's nine holes on Oahu's North Shore near Turtle Bay.

Like an uncut diamond, this rugged course has four holes running parallel to the Pacific Ocean. Built by striking Campbell Estate workers in 1946, the course has been regularly upgraded since then and play has increased, due no doubt to the low green fees.

One often hears of a golf course being described as a links-style course, but rarely do these courses resemble the true Scottish Links which wind their way through salty lowlands bordering the ocean. In this regard, Kahuku could safely be described as a links course reminiscent of the links of Scotland. Luckily, Hawaii's weather is a little better!

Kahuku has three par fives, two par fours and four par threes. Most holes are fairly straightforward. The major factor influencing play is the strong trade wind that blows almost every afternoon. Low sandhills offer little protection on the 7th and 8th holes. The 2nd, 3rd, 4th and 6th holes are directly exposed.

Dress is casual. There are handcarts but no restaurant or pro shop.

Situated on Oahu's northeast point, Kahuku is subject to strong late afternoon winds. So go early!

Superintendent:
Glenn Kakuni

For further information:
Kahuku Golf Course
P. O. Box 417
Kahuku, Oahu, HI 96731
(808) 293-5842

Ted Makalena Golf Course

Ted Makalena Golf Course, located just 20 miles from downtown Honolulu, offers perfectly straightforward golf at a reasonable price.

Designed by Bob Baldock, this 5,946-yard, par 71 course is quite flat, with few trees or bunkers. However, plenty of water runs parallel to the 6th, 7th, 14th, 15th and 16th fairways and runs right through the 17th.

Superintendent:
Heide Madrigal

For further information:
Ted Makalena Golf Course
Waipio Point Access Rd.
Waipahu, Oahu, HI 96796
(808) 671-6480

PALI GOLF COURSE

On the windward side of Oahu, right against the Koolau Mountains, just below the highway that links Oahu's two sides, is the Pali Golf Course.

Although a hometown favorite of Kailua and Kaneohe golfers, in recent years more people from Waikiki are playing at Pali, bringing play up to a high 145,000 rounds per year - that's more than 500 rounds per day. The play starts at 6.30 a.m. and players often line up from 5.30 a.m., so don't go to Pali unless you have a tee time or you could be waiting for hours.

Designed by Willard Wilkinson and opened for play in 1956, the Pali, like the Ala Wai, is taking the brunt of increases in local and tourist play. Finding a level lie is difficult on this course as it stretches from the Koolau mountains down to beautiful Kaneohe bay. The other difficulty is the numerous trees from Norfolk Pine to papaya. If it wasn't for the coconut palms and papaya you could be on a mainland mountain course. Although it does experience winds that disturb your concentration, it is the rain that interrupts play. The course was closed for sixty days last year. No matter what the conditions, the very reasonable rates will keep the traffic up on this windward course with a magnificent view.

The course is up for grabs. Franke Penne's 12-year old record of 64 still stands and the course is easier now, according to Course Superintendent, Floyd Takushi.

Superintendent:
Floyd Takushi

For further information:
Pali Golf Course
45-050 Kamehameha Hwy.
Kaneohe, Oahu, HI 96744
(808) 261-9784

OLOMANA GOLF LINKS

At Olomana, the windward trades are cool and the sun warm and inviting all year round. The clear blue ocean off eastern Oahu contrasts with the majestic Ko'olau mountain range which forms a stark and steep backdrop to the gentle rolls and hillside turns of these links.

Open to the public, this Bob Baldock design course was completed in 1969. The front nine has rolling fairways with hills and valleys, while the relatively level back nine offers the challenge of strategically placed ponds and a stream.

Though concrete cartpaths and medium speed greens ease the rounds, this is not an easy course. Tee shots often require a precise and delicate touch.

The first hole is a par 4 measuring 408 yards from the blue tees with crosswinds and a sloping fairway where distance and accuracy are crucial. Similarly, the 423-yard 16th hole is a long par 4 with water hazards left, right, and around the green. The course record at Olomana is 63 for this 6,326-yard par 72 course.

Olomana has a driving range as well as a spacious and comfortable two-story clubhouse with dining and beverage services and a well-stocked pro shop.

Reservations at this busy golf center (some 97,000 rounds yearly) are often required one month in advance.

Pro Shop Manager:
  Charlotte Clarke

For more information:
  Olomana Golf Links
  41-1801 Kalanianaole Hwy
  Waimanalo, Oahu, HI 96795
  (808) 259-7926

The Ko'olau Mountains form a majestic backdrop to the gently rolling fairways of Olomana.

HONOLULU COUNTRY CLUB

There is in business, as in golf, the necessity to put your best foot forward. To succeed in business is important and the relative measure of that attainment can be found in the membership of this very private Oahu facility known as the Honolulu Country Club. Its membership is made up of a wide ranging variety of entertainment, business and political figures and each hole on the course is named after some notable.

The course was constructed over a swampy salt lake. It was transformed in 1977 by East Coast architect, Francil Duane, aided by that inimitable sure shot, Arnold Palmer. Its 6,808 yards of sculptured beauty is basically a dry course surrounded by water. It is here that celebrities play prior to the Hawaiian Open and upwardly bound Honolulu executives work overtime. The membership is limited to 500 and there is a waiting list.

Vogels.

General Manager:
Max Muraoka

For further information:
Honolulu Country Club
1690 Ala Puumalu Street
Honolulu, Oahu, HI 96818
(808) 833-4541

HAWAII COUNTRY CLUB

The Hawaii Country Club is located in the middle of sugarcane and pineapple fields near the Waianae Mountains, some 5 miles to the southeast of Pearl Harbor and a 35 minute drive from Honolulu.

It was designed and built by Red Uldrick in 1957. In 1959, the second nine was opened. In recent years, with the golf boom, the course has become increasingly popular but still gives one a sense of country. Today, many golfers are willing to drive the 35 minutes to enjoy this course.

The 5,900 yds par 72 layout is short, hilly and very sporty. Confronting you at every turn (albeit dogleg) are monkeypod trees, some 200 of them scattered liberally through out the course.

Uldrick's whimsy reveals itself in the tree cluster 60 yards in front of the second green, the elephant ear tree on the fourth fairway, the trees at the ninth and tenth and in full force at the twelfth. The treeline crosses the entire fifteenth fairway with an opening to shoot through. This interesting use of trees and hillside necessitated the implementation of a bells and flags alert system for advancing golfers.

For further information:
Hawaii Country Club
94-1211 Kunia Road
Kunia, Oahu, HI 96786
(808) 621-5654

WAIKELE GOLF CLUB

The newest jewel among Oahu's scenic landmarks is Waikele Golf Club, an 18-hole, par 72 championship course. From every hole, players encounter distractingly beautiful vistas, sweeping from Diamond Head to the chiseled slopes of the Ko'olau mountains to the Waianae range at Waikele's back door and to the mighty blue Pacific.

Waikele is the sixth Hawaii course designed by one of America's most imaginative and respected golf architects, Ted Robinson. Robinson expects it to be one of his best. Robinson's paid special attention to the topography of the fairways and has laid down Bermuda grass that will test your skills at keeping the ball on the greens. More challenges abound in strategically placed bunkers, ponds and waterfalls. Waikele course is graced by mature coconut palms grown specifically for the course over the past 10 years.

Robinson has an affinity for water. In fact, "Water, water, everywhere" could well be Waikele's theme. The par 4 fourth hole has a dogleg left around a water feature. At the long par 3 seventeenth -- Robinson's signature hole -- the tee shot must carry a pond, with a waterfall caressing the left side of the green. The par 4 eighteenth has a beauty of a water hazard, too.

Stay out of the water and you'll find this a very playable course. Robinson says, "We wanted to create a course that makes golfers at all levels of experience yearn to come back to play again and again."

The clubhouse features a golf shop with top names in apparel and equipment, locker rooms and a restaurant. Club rentals, driving range, putting green and golf lessons are available.

Head Professional:
Melvyn Nagata

For further information:
Waikele Golf Club
94-200 Paioa Place
Waipahu, Oahu, HI 96797
(808) 676-9000

IF YOU HAVEN'T PLAYED THIS BEAUTIFUL COURSE, ISN'T IT TIME YOU TEST THE WATERS?

With cascading water features and rolling fairways to contoured greens, Waikele Golf Club is the new 18-hole, par 72 championship course to please both beginning and experienced players alike. If it's scenery that inspires you, there are sweeping views from the Ko'olau mountain range to Diamond Head and Pearl Harbor to behold. If it's challenge, there are strategically placed bunkers and intricate pin placements to keep you on your toes. And since we're located just 30 minutes west of Waikiki, it's accessible for everyone. For information call (808) 676-9000. Fax: (808) 677-9839.

WAIKELE GOLF CLUB

Waipahu, Oahu, HI

47

MILILANI GOLF CLUB

Located between the Ko'olau and Waianae mountain ranges high on the Leilehua plain in central Oahu, Mililani Golf Club is one of the few inland championship golf courses on Oahu open to the public.

Designed by course architect Bob Baldock, Mililani has been a favorite of local golfers since it opened in 1967. In recent years, the course has gained popularity among tourist golfers, especially the Japanese.

The scenic course, measuring over 6,300 yards from the regular tees, features more than enough trees, streams, ponds and gullies to make good shotmaking a priority. Wind is often a critical factor, making club selection a key to scoring well. There is also the Waiahole Ditch to contend with as it winds around half the holes on the front nine.

Mililani's first challenge is the long, 415-yard par 4 first hole. Trees line the right side of the fairway. The hole doglegs left, tempting the golfer to cut the dogleg for a shorter approach shot. But beware of a fairway bunker on the left -- it attracts golf balls like a magnet. Pull a tee shot left of the bunker and heavy rough, trees and out-of-bounds can make the first hole a tough beginning.

The 12th hole is a beautiful 165-yard par 3 that rewards an accurate iron shot to the green. The tee shot is made over a deep forested gully that winds around the front and left side of the green. If your tee shot is short or to the left, don't even bother looking for your ball. The green itself is two-tiered and slopes upward to the back, making putting difficult if you land too far below or above the flag.

For golfers who enjoy an exciting finishing hole, the 18th at Mililani is perfect. The longest par 4 on the course, this 435-yard dogleg left calls for the right club off the tee and precise placement on the fairway. Long hitters can try to cut the dogleg left, flirting with the out-of-bounds. Hitting long and to the right puts the ball into deep rough and trees. The approach requires two excellent golf shots to reach the green in regulation, avoiding two greenside bunkers and trees to the right of the green.

Mililani Golf Club is challenging enough to provide an exciting game but not to the point of frustration.

Other course facilities include a restaurant and a snack shop, a lighted driving range and a well-stocked pro shop.

Head Professional:
Jay Yasumiishi

For further information:
Mililani Golf Club
95-176 Kuahelani Ave.
Mililani, Oahu, HI 96789
(808) 623-2222

BAYVIEW GOLF CENTER

The Bayview Golf Center is a par 3 executive 18-hole golf course founded by colorful Tommy Ukauka -- three-time winner of the Hawaiian Open. Bayview was built in 1961 and is owned by Pacific Atlas Hawaii, Inc.

"This golf course gobbles balls with reckless abandon," Ukauka says, and he is not referring to the driving range. "If you're off to the right, you're in the lake. If you're on the left, you're in the river."

Bayview's two-tiered driving range is unique, as is its night golf: 18 holes, fully lit. Prices for rounds are low and the atmosphere is low-key. Come as you are. It's golf in Hawaii - Ukauka style!

Head Professional:
Tommy Ukauka

For further information:
Bayview Golf Course
45-285 Kaneohe Bay Drive
Kaneohe, Oahu, HI 96744
(808) 247-0451

MOANALUA GOLF CLUB

Long before the first resort hotel was built in Waikiki, Oahu had its first golf course. Built by Scotsman Donald MacIntyre in 1898, Moanalua was once accessible only by horse ride or streetcar and a four-mile walk.

Originally an 18 hole course, now reduced to a 9 hole 2,972 yards par 36, it is characterized by tree-lined fairways. This golf course has plenty of challenges. Holes #1 and #9 are rated as among the toughest in the state.

Supervisor:
Mark Gomes

For further information:
Moanalua Golf Club
1250 Ala Aolani St
Honolulu, Oahu, HI 96819
(808) 839-2411

Waialae Country Club

Waialae is the site of the PGA's Hawaiian Open every February. It also has the most affluent membership of any course in Hawaii. Waialae's colorful 67-year history includes being barricaded during World War II to being celebrated by Hollywood. It is, in short, the most notable golf course between California and Japan.

Waialae is located on the southeast shore of the island of Oahu, nestled among the residential homes

Waialae is the site of the annual PGA Hawaiian Open.

of Kahala. It maintains a strict private membership that includes some of the most prominent doctors, lawyers and businessmen in the state.

The eliteness of Waialae can be traced back to its opening on February 1, 1927. Originally the golf course was a concept to entice wealthy foreign interests to the Hawaiian Islands.

On November 1, 1965, under the sponsorship of United Airlines, the first PGA Hawaiian Open was played. It was won by Gay Brewer after a thrilling sudden death playoff with Bob Goalby.

A visually stunning course, Waialae offers a wide array of majestic and colorful trees, creating a separate statement on every hole. Royal Poincianas along the 11th fairway make a distracting challenge to the hole. In fact, from Pink and Queen White shower trees to the lone 150-yard marking Royal Palms, vegetation along the course is diverse.

The grass that comprises the fairways and rough is a thick common Bermuda grass, which because of a complete automatic sprinkler system, always remains green and lush. For novice golfers unaccustomed to thick rough, this is added incentive to drive the ball well or risk a buried lie in heavy grass.

The greens are a special hybrid of Bermuda called Tifdwarf, which grows well in open sunlight but demands constant observation. The greens are so well-manicured that many touring golf professionals feel they are, indeed, the best greens on tour, and Waialae's perfect greens condition is a prime reason the pros shoot the low scores they do every year. Not blazing fast, but usually considered slick, most of the greens have testy undulations, increased in difficulty by the prevailing trade winds.

Of all the golf courses on the island of Oahu, Waialae remains a distinct and traditional icon, comparable to none, yet as challenging as any. Throughout the last two decades, most of the club's facilities have been remodeled to a grander scale. However, they are restricted to club membership. Members are allowed to bring one playing guest per round, but during some restricted times, up to three are permissible. The golf pro shop is fully stocked and is open 7 days a week.

The club also has a driving range available to members and their guests, open during daylight hours only. Golf balls are free, but only irons can be hit. No woods are allowed. Fast play is also a requirement at the course -- no rounds of 18 holes over four hours are tolerated.

Head Professional:
Greg Nichols

For further information:
Waialae Country Club
4997 Kahala Avenue
Honolulu, Oahu, HI 96816
(808) 732-1457

Wind, water and narrow fairways make West Loch one of Oahu's most challenging municipal courses.

WEST LOCH MUNICIPAL GOLF COURSE

On the southwest side of Pearl Harbor, approximately 30 minutes from Waikiki, sits the newest of the five municipal courses on the island of Oahu. The 18-hole, par 72 West Loch Golf Course opened for play in early 1990 and quickly gained popularity in a state where the demand for tee times greatly outstrips the supply. The course measures 6,615 yards from the back tees.

Getting a tee time can be difficult on many courses on Oahu, and this is particularly true on the municipal courses. To have a chance of obtaining a starting time, you must try to book West Loch one week in advance. If you're playing solo, try walking on in the morning and you might be on the course by noon.

West Loch Golf Course was the first municipal course to open on Oahu since the nearby Ted Makalena Course opened over 20 years ago. It is one of the most challenging of the island's municipal courses. West Loch sits in the midst of a residential housing area, West Loch Estates, and utilizes the natural layout of the land to the fullest extent.

The low elevation of the back nine is bordered by the far western reaches of Pearl Harbor and requires extensive water drainage. Taking advantage of this, drainage ditches and runoff ponds act as hazards on several holes.

It is an unusual layout in that the 1st hole plays right in front of the clubhouse, but then you have to drive under an expressway which divides the course to reach the 2nd hole. You play holes 2 through 11 on this side of the highway, then switch back through the tunnel to play the final seven holes.

Being a newer course, the vegetation is still maturing and the fairways can be hard in some places.

Water hazards come into play on quite a number of holes, with the 2nd and the 11th sharing a large fairway lake, as do the 12th and 17th.

There are no shortage of beautiful vistas at West Loch, as the panorama stretches from distant downtown Honolulu on one side to the green cliffs of the Waianae Mountains on the other.

Wind is a factor on most holes, and combined with the narrow fairways found on certain parts of the layout, wind strength is one of the factors that makes West Loch challenging.

To help prepare you for the abundance of water on this course, West Loch has built an unusual water driving range -- a lake into which your practice balls splash when they descend. Nelson and Wright, the team who designed West Loch, say this was the only practical solution to the lay of the land.

To get to West Loch, take the H-1 Freeway west from Honolulu for approximately half an hour. Take the Ewa exit, which is also posted as Highway 76. Loop back toward the ocean and the west loch of Pearl Harbor for which the area was named. Stay in the left lane and turn left at West Loch Estates, just opposite St. Francis West Medical Center. Take two immediate turns and park.

Golf Professional:
 Ty Otake

For further information:
West Loch Golf Course
91-1126 Okupa Street
Ewa Beach, HI 96706
(808) 676-2210

HAWAII KAI GOLF COURSES

Situated approximately 16 miles from the heart of Waikiki, this golf course is getting lots of play these days, particularly with the new influx of Japanese golfers.

Actually, this is not one course but two. The Hawaii Kai Championship course is a 6,600 yards par 72 course designed by William (Billy) Bell. Bell uses both water and sand to make this course a challenge.

The 7th is the number one handicap hole. It is a 395 yard par 4 from the white tee that requires the driver to lay up short so that the next shot will carry a water hazard to the right. To the left is out of bounds. The green is undulating. This is a deserving number one handicap hole.

The 14th hole, 505 yards from the men's tee, is a long uphill par 5 dogleg right with out-of-bounds on both sides of the fairway. There are two bunkers on the left and one to the right waiting to bury your drive. The green is heavily protected by four bunkers leaving little clear passage. The wind can become a factor, particularly in the late afternoon.

Although Hawaii Kai receives maximum play, the fairways and greens are kept in the best condition.

The Hawaii Kai Executive Golf Course was actually built 11 years after the Championship course, with design by the world's foremost golf course architect, Robert Trent Jones, Sr. At 2,433 yards, this short course is a par 55, with the emphasis on chipping and putting. The course gets plenty of use not only by the busy executive but also by the inexperienced golfer wishing to sharpen skills before playing on a full-size course.

Whichever course you play, the drive to Hawaii Kai from Waikiki is magnificent. The road twists and winds around craters and cliffs, affording views of Koko Head, the Kamapuu Cliffs and the beautiful Pacific Ocean.

The clubhouse at Hawaii Kai has an excellent full service pro shop and a second floor restaurant. The lighted driving range has an adjoining snack bar. Resevations for tee times are essential on weekends and holidays.

Head Professional:
John Inzer

For further information:
Hawaii Kai Golf Courses
8902 Kalanianaole Hwy
Honolulu, Oahu, HI 96825
(808) 395-2358

Carry water and avoid a bunker to make the green on Hawaii Kai's 13th.

BIG ISLAND

Course	No. of holes	Yardage	Rating	Par	Golf Cart Mandatory?	Cart Fees	Club Rental	Pro Shop	Driving Range	Night Lights	Restaurant	Cocktails	Green Fees	Course type
Hamakua Country Club	9	M: 2520	64.5	33	no	n/a	no	no	no	no	no	yes	$10/day	M
Hapuna Golf Course Mauna Kea Resort	18	Ch: 6875 M: 6534 W: 5067	72.1 69.9 63.9	72 72 72	yes	included	yes	yes	yes	no	yes	yes	Resort $80 Public $130	R
Hilo Municipal Golf Course	18	Ch: 6325 M: 6006 W: 5034	70.4 68.8 69.1	72 72 72	no	$12.50	yes	yes	yes	yes	yes	yes	Wkday $6 Wkend $8	M
Kona Country Club	18	Ch: 6579 M: 6155 W: 5499	71.7 69.1 70.3	72 72 73	yes	included	yes	yes	yes	no	yes	yes	Resort $60 Public $100 Guest $65	R
(Ali'i Course)	18	Ch: 6471 M: 5828 W: 4906	71.5 68.7 69.2	72 72 72	yes	included	yes	yes	yes	no	yes	yes	Resort $60 Public $100 Guest $65	R
Makalei Hawaii Country Club	18	Ch: 7091 M: 6698 W: 5242	73.5 71.4 64.9	72 72 72	yes	included	yes	yes	yes	no	yes	yes	Resort $70 Public $110	PU
Mauna Kea Golf Course Mauna Kea Resort	18	Ch: 7114 M: 6365 W: 5277	73.6 70.1 69.6	72 72 72	yes	included	yes	yes	yes	no	yes	yes	Resort $80 Public $130	R
Mauna Lani Resort (Francis H. I'i Brown Courses -- South Course)	18	Ch: 7029 M: 6370 W: 5331	73.2 70.3 70.3	72 72 72	yes	included	yes	yes	yes	no	yes	yes	Resort $65 Public $130	R
Mauna Lani Resort (Francis H. I'i Brown Courses -- North Course)	18	Ch: 6993 M: 6361 W: 5474	73.1 70.2 71.4	72 72 72	yes	included	yes	yes	yes	no	yes	yes	Resort $65 Public $130	R
Naniloa Country Club	9	M: 5610 W: 5285	65.8 69.6	70 70	no	$7	yes	no	yes	yes	no	no	Wkday $25 Wkend $35	PU
Sea Mountain at Punalu'u	18	Ch: 6492 M: 6106 W: 5663	72.0 69.7 71.5	72 72 72	yes	included	yes	yes	yes	no	yes	yes	Public $50	PU
Volcano Golf and Country Club	18	Ch: 6270 M: 5965 W: 5499	70.4 68.6 70.7	72 72 72	yes	included	yes	yes	yes	yes	yes	yes	Public $50	PU
Waikoloa Golf Club (King's Course)	18	Ch: 6594 M: 6010 W: 5459	71.3 68.6 71.0	72 72 72	yes	included	yes	yes	yes	no	no	no	Resort $80 Public $95	R
Waikoloa Golf Club (Beach Course)	18	Ch: 6566 M: 5958 W: 5094	71.5 68.6 69.4	72 72 72	yes	included	yes	yes	yes	no	yes	yes	Resort $80 Public $95	R
Waikoloa Village Golf Course	18	Ch: 6791 M: 6230 W: 5479	71.8 69.2 72.1	72 72 72	no	$15	yes	yes	yes	no	yes	yes	Public $50	R
Waimea Golf Course	18	Ch: 6661 M: 6210 W: 5673	--- --- ---	72 72 72	no	included	yes	yes	yes	no	no	yes	Not Avail.	PU

R = RESORT   PR = PRIVATE
PU = PUBLIC   M = MUNICIPAL
ALL RATES SUBJECT TO CHANGE

ALOHA BIG ISLAND

Hawaii, also known as the "Big Island", is the latest and largest addition to the Hawaiian archipelago. Molten lava still flows from Kilauea to the sea, where it solidifies and increases the island's land mass continually.

Mauna Loa, the world's largest volcano, looms 13,680 feet above sea level and 32,000 feet from the seabed, making it also the highest mountain on earth. Mauna Kea, a now dormant volcano, rises to a height of 13,796 feet and in winter its snowcapped peaks can be seen as far away as Haleakala on Maui.

In designing the Mauna Kea Golf Course, Robert Trent Jones Sr. literally hacked out acres of solid rock and crushed it to a powdery consistency, turning a lava wasteland into a spectacular layout voted recently by Golf Digest in the Top 12 of America's Finest Golf Resorts.

One of Hawaii's newest courses is the five-star Hapuna Golf Course, winner of a Golf Magazine 1992 "Top Ten Award for New Courses in the Nation". The second course to open adjacent to Mauna Kea, Hapuna was designed to provide play for the Hapuna Beach Prince Hotel, scheduled to open in the near future. Designed by Arnold Palmer and Ed Seay, this links-style course has multiple tee placements allowing a golfer to choose according the the level of his or her game.

Also on the sunny Kohala Coast, the Mauna Lani Resort was built right on top of a lava flow at the ocean's edge. The South Course offers golf on a "moonscape", while on the North Course, trees are more of a factor. However, if your balls go out-of-bounds on either course, they will be seen bouncing off the lava several times before disappearing into cracks in the lava bed.

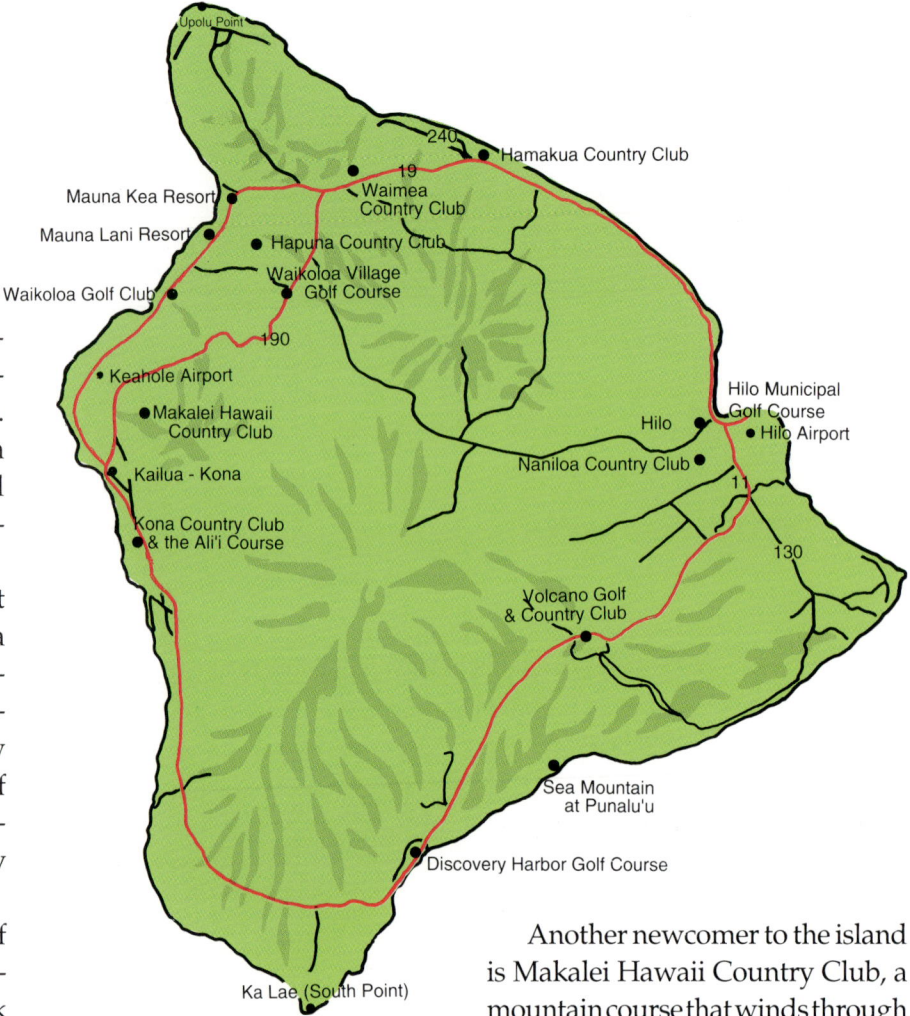

Ten miles from the picturesque town of Kailua is Kona Country Club, which has grown from 9 to 27 holes over the past two decades. Recently, it has been redesigned into two eighteens -- the Kona Country Club and The Ali'i Country Club. Kona is comprised of two ocean nines, while the Ali'i consists of the original Mauka nine plus a new nine added in 1991. Significantly tougher than the ocean course, the Ali'i eighteen has outstanding views reminiscent of the Hawaii of old.

Another newcomer to the island is Makalei Hawaii Country Club, a mountain course that winds through native oak tree forests and inactive lava tubes at a cool 1,500 feet elevation. Here they have taken great care to preserve the natural beauty of the native Hawaiian flora, re-establishing many species of indigenous trees and plants.

Even further inland is Waimea Country Club which opened at the end of 1993. This "upcountry" course has a pastoral environment quite unlike the coastal resort courses, as it winds through dairy pastures and giant stands of ironwood, eucalyptus and pine trees.

All in all, there are a total of 16 golf courses to choose from on the Big Island of Hawaii. The range of golf is complete, as is the range of weather and temperatures. A trip to this dramatic island is unforgettable and like nothing else in the world.

KONA COUNTRY CLUB & THE ALI'I COUNTRY CLUB

Kona Country Club lies on the Big Island's western coastal slopes ten minutes from the picturesque town of Kailua. Being on the lee side of the island, Kona gets very little rain and the wind is blocked by 13,680 feet of solid lava called Mauna Kea.

Kona Country Club, which has grown from nine to 27 holes over the past two decades, has recently been redesigned into two eighteens, the Kona Country Club and the Ali'i Country Club. An avid golfer will find the complex offers a full range of challenges.

Architect William Bell, Sr. designed the original nine of the Kona Country Club, now called the Ocean Back, just north of the existing clubhouse. In 1974, the Ocean Front and the hotel were built and in 1985 the Mauka (or mountain side) nine opened.

Kona Country Club is comprised of the two ocean nines. The 6,579-yard, par 72 course is quite popular. The wider, flatter fairways afford a quick, easy style of play that is characteristic of resort golf courses. However, the greens can fool you. When the weather is dry, they are fast.

The third hole on the ocean front is definitely a challenge. Although it is rated a 17 handicap hole, head professsional Rob Wohlgemuth points out, "If there is any wind at the Kona Country Club it is a light breeze from the ocean, so you have to take that into account. Also, lava comes right into the middle of the fairway and when the surf is high, the spray can hit you in the face." The overall view may be a distraction from golf but it is also a unique attraction.

The Ali'i Country Club is made up of the original Mauka nine plus a new nine, designed by the team of Robin Nelson and Rodney Wright and added in 1991. The Ali'i name was given to the course in honor of the great Hawaiian monarch King Kamehameha III, who was born in nearby Keauhou Bay. The King held sports events on this land, including a dangerous game of mud sliding, in which warriors would lie on long wooden slides and descend the mountain at fantastic speeds, sometimes losing their lives in the process. The Royal Holua Slide is a historic landmark and is located near the 13th fairway.

The Ali'i eighteen is far more challenging than the ocean course, with narrower fairways and harder-to-read greens. As the course continues to mature and the trees that line the fairways grow taller, the Ali'i eighteen will get tougher still.

The view is also outstanding. However, when there are volcanic eruptions, a haze called "vog" (volcanic smog) tends to dull colors and reminds one of Los Angeles rather than Hawaii.

For golfers used to mountain courses, the Ali'i Country Club will be like an old friend. Unlike

Kona Surf Hotel in the background

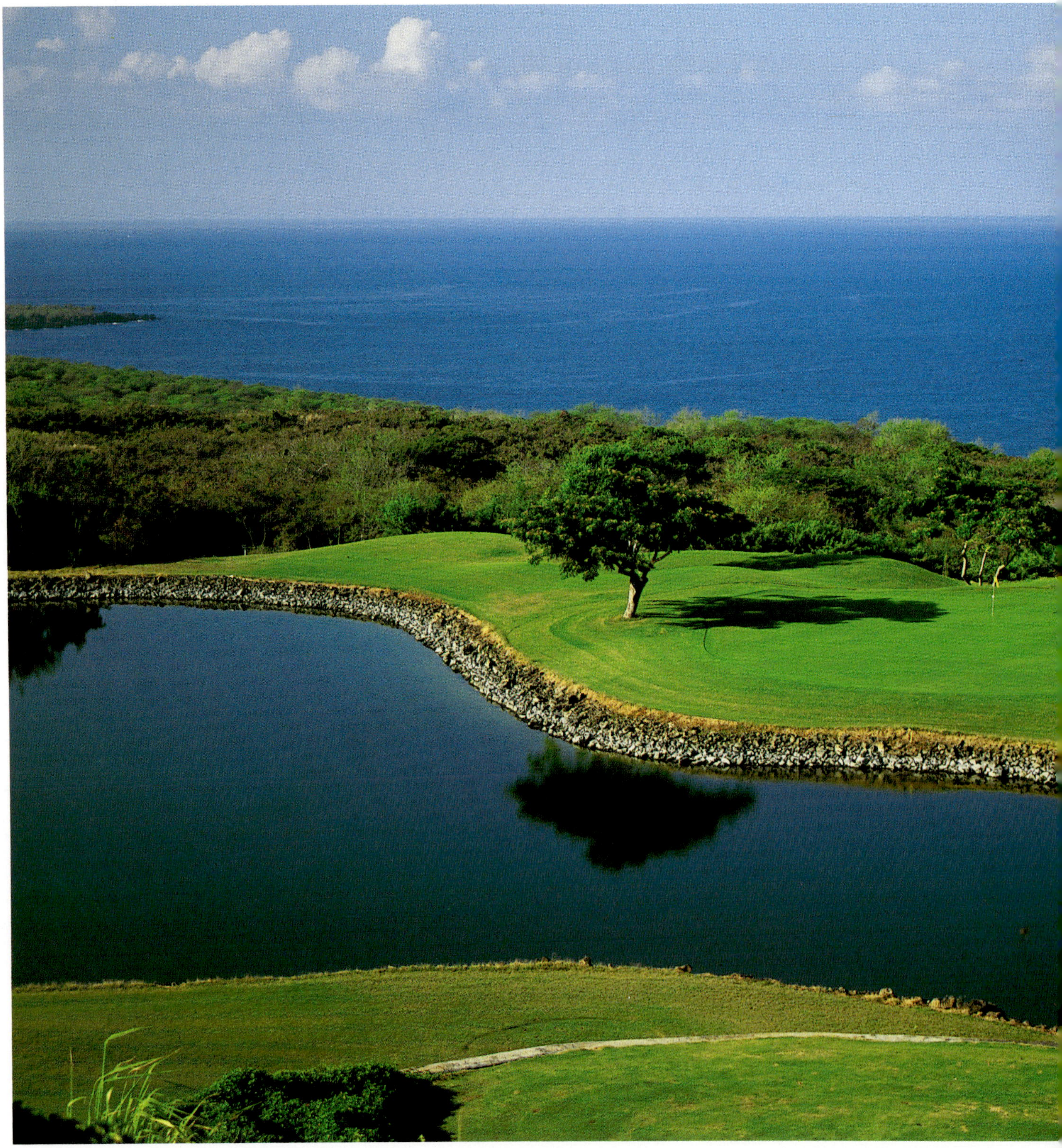

the relatively flat topography of the ocean-side Kona eighteen, the uplands Ali'i course has a more complex layout, and requires each hole to be read individually.

The Ali'i seventh hole is a typical example. At 500 yards from the white tee, it is a difficult par 4 because of a very narrow landing area for your tee shot. It is difficult to see where you want to land. In fact from the championship tee, you have to walk up to the base and look down. Next to the green is a small lake and beyond the green is a very steep slope. If you go over the top you are gone. It is all grass but it will go all the way down. Sometimes, you will hit the cart path and the ball keeps going toward the 8th green.

"The best way to play," says Wohlgemuth, "is straight down the middle but that is difficult because of the slope." The best bet is to play a one or two iron off the tee. Your tee shot will roll down the hill and from there you will be in pretty good shape. The average player will want to play up short and hope his wedge is working. A five for this hole is acceptable.

The Nelson-Wright team has designed the new back nine to be different from the front nine. Fairways, although on the side of a dormant volcano, are designed with less break to the ocean than the front nine. Shots should find their way to relatively flat areas. Compared to the front nine, the fairways are more undulating and are bordered by mature trees that remain from original forest cover.

The Ali'i 13th and 14th holes are ones to appreciate. A gentle dogleg right, the 13th is a par 5 measuring 479 yards from the white tees. With a grassy bunker on the left and deep sand to the right, you will want to aim toward the monkeypod tree on the right side to be safe. The rest is all uphill!

The 14th is a gem. A 149-yard par 3, this hole drops 110 yards from the tee to the green. The most common mistake is to misjudge the distance and use too much club. The error is all the more understandable when one needs to clear the water guarding the front of the green and the single bunker to the right. The view from the tee to the south is truly magnificent, with no development or buildings in sight -- a quick flashback to the Hawaii of old.

A single clubhouse services both courses and houses the Vista Restaurant, open for breakfast and lunch. Discount rates on play are available to those who stay at the adjacent Kona Surf Hotel.

Head Professional:
Rob Wohlgemuth

For further information:
Kona Country Club &
The Ali'i Country Club
78-7000 Alii Drive
Kailua-Kona, Hawaii,
HI 96740
(808) 322-2595

The Ali'i Course 12th hole.

WAIMEA COUNTRY CLUB

The Big Island of Hawaii is already known as a golfer's paradise. In the latter part of 1993, Waimea Country Club opened and the Big Island's reputation for first-class golf got that much bigger.

Located near the quaint town of Waimea, in an area known for its beef cattle, eucalyptus and Norfolk pine trees, Waimea Country Club is open for club members from Japan and for public play.

This John Sanford-designed course measures 6,210 yards from the blue tees. The tees and greens are bent grass and the fairways are kukui grass mixed with rye grass. The course winds through dairy pastures and giant stands of ironwood, eucalyptus and pine trees. The winds are northeast and do come into play, but the holes that face the wind are rather short. The winds can and will reach 20 mph from time to time.

The 5th hole is a par 4, measuring 394 yards from the blue tee, and is a slight dogleg right. Ball placement is critical on this hole. Your drive must take into account a reservoir that is situated just before the green. Your second shot must clear that reservoir. There is another reservoir on your left and a large sand bunker on your right, sandwiching a narrow entrance to the green. The green is large and elevated, with a sharp drop-off into the reservoir on your left-hand side. The green breaks left to right and toward the front of the green.

The 10th hole is a 396-yard par 4. The drive is downhill from an elevated tee and the wind is in your face, so this hole plays long. The hole is a dogleg with two sand bunkers on your left and right. From the tee the green is blind, but in fact the opening is quite wide. Your first shot will take you parallel to the sand on a fairway that breaks toward the ocean from right to left. You're shooting to a small, undulating green that breaks from back to front.

Waimea's signature hole is the 480-yard 16th, a par 5. The wind is generally behind your right shoulder, going across the fairway. There is a water hazard on the left, a sand bunker farther up on your left at about 230 yards, and another bunker at the end of the fairway. The entrance to the green is off to the right of the green so at some point you may need to cut corners to get to the green. The idea would be to keep to the right of the fairway so you can cut the corner to the green on your third shot.

Waimea Country Club is an "upcountry" course, with a pastoral environment that is a departure from the resort courses along the coast. The course clubhouse, while not elaborate, is quite nice. An expanded clubhouse and facilities are planned.

For more information:
Waimea Country Club
P.O. Box 2155
Kamuela, Hawaii, HI 96743
(808) 885-8777

Giant stands of ironwood, eucalyptus and pine trees are a feature -- and a hazard -- of Waimea Country Club.

The Best of Both Worlds

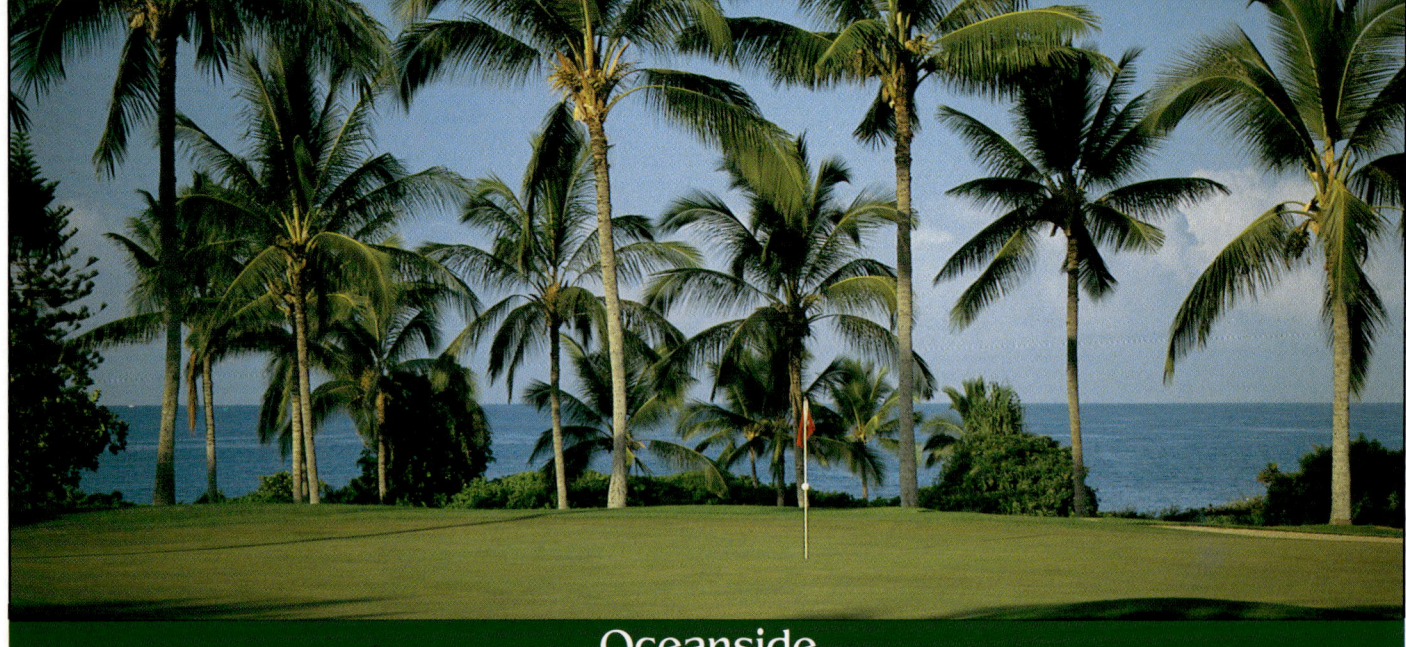

Oceanside
KONA COUNTRY CLUB

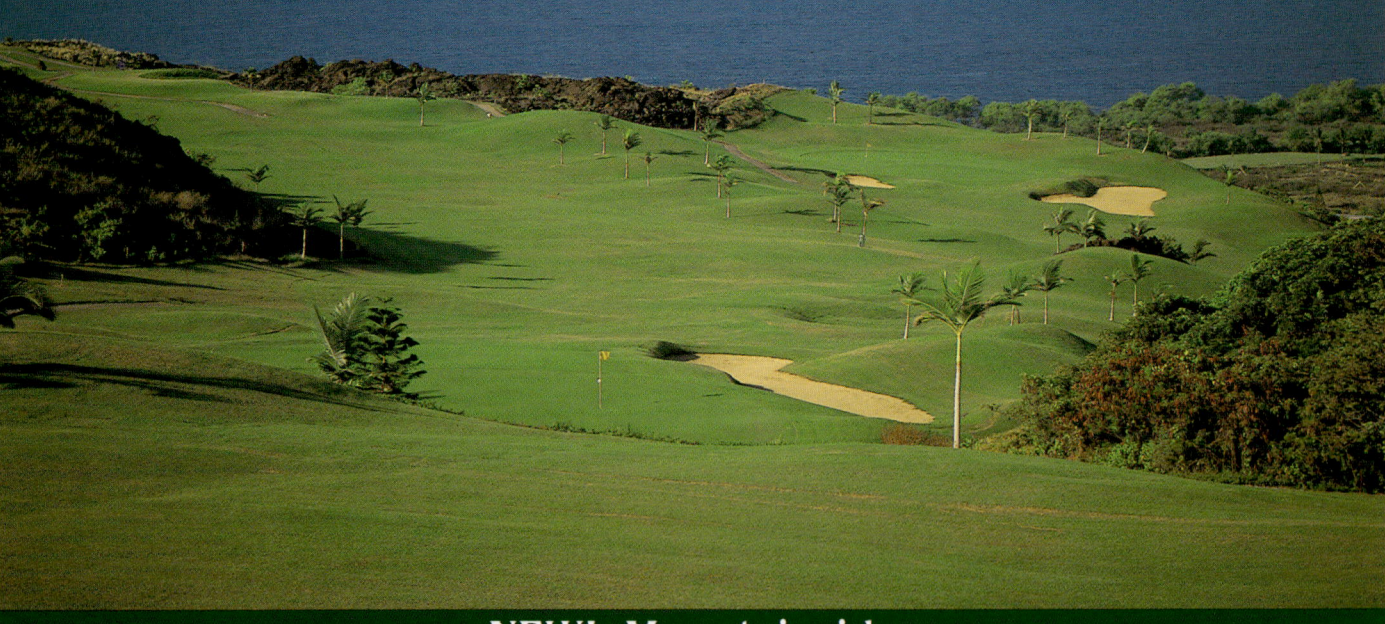

NEW! Mountainside
ALI'I COUNTRY CLUB

Kona Country Club -- Eighteen holes border the ocean with lush open fairways, fast and true manicured greens, rugged ancient lava flows and stunning panoramas of the blue Pacific.

Ali'i Country Club -- A challenging new eighteen winds its way through Big Island uplands with narrow fairways, multiple-break greens and outstanding mountain and ocean views.

Either way, you'll enjoy the sunny perfection of the Big Island's leeward coast, the total convenience of a well-equipped clubhouse and the tasty delights of breakfast and lunch at our Vista Restaurant, overlooking Keauhou Bay.

Kona Country Club & The Ali'i Country Club
78-7000 Ali'i Drive, Kailua-Kona, Hawaii 96740
(808) **322-2595**

KCC Hawaii
Kona Country Club

Palmer and Seay used the contours of old lava flows to create an undulating, links style course at Hapuna.

HAPUNA GOLF COURSE

On the Big Island's Kohala Coast (which should be renamed the "Golf Coast") is another five-star golf course garnering recognition.

Designed by Arnold Palmer and Ed Seay, Hapuna Golf Course was a winner of a <u>Golf</u> Magazine 1992 "Top Ten Award for New Courses in the Nation," and was named "Most Environmentally Sensitive" of Hawaii's courses and "the Course of the Future" by the U.S. Golf Association.

Hapuna is the second course to open adjacent to the Mauna Kea Resort. The Mauna Kea Golf Course needs little introduction, having won many coveted awards and an international reputation. While the temptation may be to draw comparison between the two, they are so different that it is not easy to draw quick conclusions. Suffice to say that Hapuna Golf Course was designed to complement the Mauna Kea Golf Course and to provide play for the Hapuna Beach Prince Hotel. It is experiencing popularity with visitors and Hawaii's local golfing population.

What Palmer and Seay have done is to use the natural flow and contours of the land to provide a gently undulating link-style course overlooking the Kohala Coast. Hapuna takes full advantage of great views, from majestic Mauna Kea volcanic peak with the peaceful Kohala Mountains in the foreground, to the broad blue Pacific stretching across the horizon. At 6,029 yards from the regular tees, it cannot be described as long. However, if the wind is from the north, the course can play extremely long with many uphill, into-the-wind shots. The course is designed for the prevalent 5 to 7 mph sea breeze that is usually just enough to cool you from the midday sun.

PGA Golf Pro Ron Castillo, Jr. (of a famous Hawaii golfing fam-

The Big Island's indigenous vegetation makes Hapuna a beautiful and challenging course.

ily) pointed out several singular facts about Hapuna. Since building the golf course, the native bird population has more than tripled. Don't be surprised to see pheasants or the state bird, the Nene Goose, roaming the thick pili grass which is the predominant vegetation here. Other indigenous flora include kiawe trees and sweet-smelling ilima bushes.

Castillo also explained that "hapuna" means "spouting water." Underground streams run through Hapuna Golf Course and empty into the bay at such velocity it makes the ocean spout at the stream's entrance. This is the basis of Hapuna's logo design.

Hapuna's tee markers are made of kiawe logs (an indigenous prickly tree related to the mesquite) in imitation of the pine logs used at Augusta National. Like many new resort courses, Hapuna has multiple tee placements, allowing a golfer to choose according to the level of his game.

The first hole is a 511-yard par 5 with a dogleg left. The dogleg is narrow and funnels between two small hills. The tee shot should be played down the left side to cut the angle and to take advantage of the downhill roll. With a good drive and the help of a sea breeze, the large green will tempt the low handicap golfer to make it in two.

However, beware of the water on the right. For the short shooter there are three bunkers waiting on the right about 30 yards before the green. Watch out for those Hawaiian water fowl on this hole.

There are two types of bunkers at Hapuna Golf Course. Those with green rakes represent a hazard; those with orange rakes represent transitional bunkers. You may ground your club and remove loose impediments on transitional bunkers.

The 7th hole is 135 yards from the regular tee, slightly uphill and is guarded by a transitional bunker from tee to green. The bunker should not come into play -- but as we all know, it wasn't put there for nothing!

On many holes at Hapuna Golf Course, the tee boxes are surrounded by natural vegetation. This results in many lost balls, so stock up before you hit the links. According to talk at the pro shop, one couple lost 25 balls between them!

Once you cross the highway to play the 1st and the 18th holes, the topography undergoes a striking transformation from rough, arid conditions to lush palm-fringed fairways similar to the Mauna Kea Golf Course. The recently completed clubhouse and driving range are located here.

The 350-room, all ocean-view Hapuna Beach Prince Hotel features a number of non-golf amenities, including a complete health and fitness center, tennis courts and five restaurants offering a variety of menus.

Hapuna is an excellent new golf course. Golf Magazine, in selecting Hapuna for a 1992 "Top Ten New Courses" award, said it best: "subtle, traditional designs that emphasize strategy are in; the 'jagged edge' school of exaggerated effect and impending disaster is out ... stringent environmental laws have forced the creation of compact layouts that tiptoe through sensitive areas and test accuracy to the maximum."

Hapuna Golf Course is a perfect getaway for Oahu's crowded golfing population or for visitors staying in the surrounding resorts who want a change from their resort's golf courses.

Golf Professional:
Ron Castillo, Jr.

For further information:
Hapuna Golf Course
Kohala Coast,
Hawaii, HI 96743-9706
(808) 882-1035

The ninth hole is touched by the golden light of the setting sun.

MAUNA KEA

It was love at first sight. The drive from Queen Kaahumanu Highway to Mauna Kea presented a scene of contrasts. Black lava, the color of licorice, suddenly turns to green fairways, palms and white beaches. When they created Mauna Kea, they combined a multitude of elements and built a course and a resort that is simply a pleasure to visit. Mauna Kea is ranked among "America's 100 Greatest" golf courses and as "Hawaii's finest" by Golf Digest and more recently voted in the top 12 of America's finest golf resorts. Course architect, Robert Trent Jones, Sr. describes Mauna Kea as "one of our greatest opportunities (of converting) lava wasteland into a spectacular layout on which we have grown a grass as fine as you can find anywhere".

Greens and fairways had to be literally hacked out of the acres of solid lava rock. An elaborate automatic underground watering system was developed to supplement the meager rainfall. It pumps over a million gallons of water per day. To solve the problem of no topsoil, Robert Trent Jones, Sr. decided to make his own. He brought in heavy equipment and crushed the volcanic rock to a powdery consistency through repeated grading and rolling. Hundreds of coconut palms and other trees including rainbow shower, wili-wili, monkey pod and Chinese banyan were brought in to accent the landscaping. The project was completed in 1964. Jones describes it as one of his crowning achievements and we agree.

The surrounding views are nothing short of spectacular. Rising from the sea are the twin peaks of Mauna Kea and Mauna Loa, two of the world's highest mountains. Skirting the shore is one of the prettiest white sand beaches and the bluest, clearest ocean. There is nothing like an island in the middle of the Pacific. Although it is nearly 2,000 years since the Polynesian voyagers landed on Ka Lae (South Point) and more than 2 centuries since Captain Cook landed at Kealakekua Bay on the Island of Hawaii, the clarity of the air and water and the white sand beaches still exists in this modern age.

Architect Jones created a course that reflects his philosophy that "every hole should be a demanding par and a comfortable bogey". This was achieved through the use of undulating fairways, uphill holes, steep greens, doglegs and

Mauna Kea's fairways are excellent in both design and maintenance.

strategically placed bunkers. The course has 120 bunkers in all, nearly twice that of a typical course. Despite the 52,000 rounds played each year, the greens and fairways are kept in excellent condition by Robert Itamoto, one of golf's finest green superintendents.

The third hole is considered one of Mauna Kea's most difficult. It is certainly one of the most photographed. This par 3 hole is 210 yards from the black tee to 180 from the red. Between you and the hole is the Pacific Ocean, sometimes calm as a mill pond, at other times whipped into a fury by large southwest swells. The green is fast, slightly elevated and guarded by bunkers. You can play to the right a bit into a safer area and still make par. The secret to this hole is easy to identify and hard to achieve. All you have to do is ignore the ocean. Act like it's not there and if you can't, bring plenty of balls!

Hole eleven is also a par 3. It plays 247 yards from the black tee and 208 from the blue. It is considered to be the most difficult hole on the course, averaging well over four strokes. The shot is a long one from a 100 foot elevation to the green below. There is a falling-off on three sides. If your ball lands on the right or left and rolls down into the trees, you may end up making six, seven or eight strokes. From the black tee, you're looking at 247 yards downhill, so it's probably about 230 yards. If there's any wind at all, you're looking at a wood and it gets pretty scary when you play a wood into such a small target. It looks like a pretty big green, but it's not really, because of the way it drops off. When Nicklaus played here in four competitive rounds in the Big 3, he never hit the green and never made a par on this hole. So if you make par, put another feather in your cap!

One nice thing about Mauna Kea is that it is not overly affected by wind. Statistics kept by Mauna Kea show they have between 28 to 52 days of wind and the rest of the time there is a 5 to 7 mph breeze. As far as rain is concerned, Mauna Kea has been closed four times in 23 years. The course gets 6 to 8 inches of rain a year, mainly in the evenings.

Mauna Kea Resort is owned by Seibu Corporation, which also owns the Makena Golf Course on Maui. Fortunately for golfers, Seibu is maintaining Mauna Kea as one of the world's finest golf courses!

Director of Golf:
Joe Root

For further information:
Mauna Kea Golf Course
1 Mauna Kea Beach Drive
Kohala Coast,
Hawaii, HI 96743-9706
(808) 882-7222

The 376-yard, handicap 7 first hole is a great way to start your day.

MAKALEI HAWAII COUNTRY CLUB

The most recent addition to the golf scene on the Big Island of Hawaii is not the palm-fringed ocean course one has come to expect in recent years. Instead, Makalei Hawaii Country Club is a mountain course that winds through native oak tree forests and inactive lava tubes at an elevation of 1,500 feet. Makalei's high altitude location not only makes for cool play on a hot day but also provides protection from the strong winds that sometimes bedevil play on the ocean-side courses of the Big Island.

Designed by Dick Nugent, the Makalei Hawaii Country Club is a par 72, eighteen-hole championship course, measuring 7,091 yards from the championship tees with a rating of 73.5 and 6,698 yards from the blues with a rating of 71.4.

Makalei sports four holes straight up the slope and five straight down. The rest run laterally to the mountain slope. The fairways are undulating, so overall this course demands careful club choice and accurate ball positioning.

The 1st hole prepares you for the challenges. A straight fairway fringed by trees rises at about a 30-degree angle to a medium-sized green guarded by three bunkers. This is not a complicated first hole, but it does teach you to club up or you won't make the distance you think. A par 4 at 222 yards from the blue tee, you can make a clubbing mistake and still make par.

The 3rd hole is a tricky dogleg left par 4. For the long hitter, a good drive aimed at the center of the fairway will probably put you

into rough that infringes on the fairway's right. Better to go left and cut the corner on the dogleg. This will give you a good roll toward the elevated green.

The 385-yard 8th hole, a par 4, features a green guarded by a grass bunker on the left and a sand bunker with a large lava tube on the right. From this vantage point, there are views of the Kohala Coast extending miles into the distance.

The 9th hole is a par 4 at 342 yards from the blue tee that requires a high tee shot to clear the rough immediately in front of the box. The short hitter will be hard put to make the green in two. Watch for the lava tube at the back of the green.

From the tee box of the 17th hole, the golfer has a feeling of power. At 404 yards from the blue tee, the undulating fairway is all downhill to a smallish green backed by Hawaiian oak trees.

From here, your big drive can take you a lot more than halfway there. Watch for the bunker on the right.

Although a new course, the fairways and greens are in remarkably good shape, appearing maturer than most courses many years older. The greens themselves are bent grass and play true and fair. You can make putts you normally miss -- a real ego boost for some of us!

This challenging golf course also has a social conscience and places a high priority on the preservation of native Hawaiian flora and fauna.

Makalei has re-established many species of indigenous trees and native plants which flourish within the course's elevation range of 2,100 to 2,800 feet above sea level. The diverse flora gracing the landscape of Makalei include *koa*, *kukui*, *mamane* and *ohia* trees, as well as the rare *iliahi*, or sandalwood tree. *Ohia lehua* and other ferns and native flowers are visible throughout the course.

Ohia and *koa* trees have been planted in the area from the State Forest, south of the 12th green, to the boundary with Hualalai Ranch, north of the 10th tee. These trees provide a natural fly-way for birds.

Among the native birds sometimes visible are the *i'o*, a Hawaiian hawk; the *pue'o*, an owl; and the *i'iwi*. The canary finch, meadowlark, peacock and Chinese ringneck pheasant are among the introduced species which have made Makalei their home.

Makalei's efforts to preserve and enhance the natural beauty of the Hawaiian environment are a testament to the fact that people and nature can co-exist.

Makalei Hawaii Country Club includes a clubhouse, a well-stocked pro shop and a restaurant and lounge.

Situated only 15 to 20 minutes from Keohole Airport, Makalei's convenient location is a great asset.

For further information:
Makalei Hawaii Country Club
72-3890 Hawaii Belt Road
Kailua-Kona, Hawaii, HI 96740
(808) 325-6625

Golf Above The Rest

The 17th hole

Makalei Hawaii Country Club

Treat yourself to 18 holes of par 72 championship golf 2,000 feet above the blue Pacific Ocean in the un-paralleled beauty and climate above Kona's Gold Coast at Makalei Hawaii. Discover the serenity of Hawaii's pre-eminent course with bent-grass greens where the views are as spectacular as the golf action!

Discover golf at its best. For tee times & information, call:

1-800-606-9606
or **(808) 325-6625**

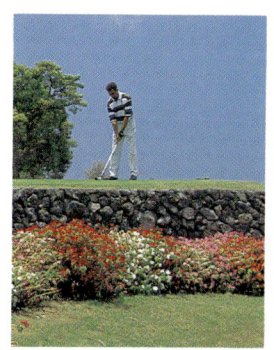

Makalei Hawaii Country Club   72-3890 Hawaii Belt Road   Kailua-Kona, HI U.S.A. 96740

WAIKOLOA GOLF CLUB

Another amazing feat of Hawaiian engineering and architecture, the Waikoloa Golf Club was literally carved out of solid lava on the shores of spectacular Anaeho'omalu Bay.

The whole area is steeped in Hawaiian history, legend and folklore and none of the historically significant areas were disturbed in the course's construction. Hawaii's second largest petroglyph field is located between the 6th and 7th holes. Ancient burial caves are located at the end of the driving range and the remains of an ancient fishing village are still standing right in the middle of the 12th fairway.

Waikoloa Golf Club is composed of two eighteens, the Beach Course and the King's Course. Golfing conditions are exceptional -- a typical Hawaiian 80 degrees most of the year with only seven to ten inches of rain annually and most of that occurring at night. The wind plays an important part here, as in many other Hawaii courses.

The Beach Course, designed by Robert Trent Jones, Jr., was created in 1981 as a 6,003-yard, par 70 course. After extensive renovation in 1989 it now measures 6,507 yards from the championship tees and 5,920 yards from the resort tees. The course bears Jones, Jr.'s trademarks of narrow, gently rolling fairways, tight doglegs and elevated tees. Jones has increased the challenge of the Beach Course by adding 76 bunkers and three lakes.

Challenge on the back nine starts on the 364-yard 10th hole. This par 4 doglegs right to a well-bunkered green with a cove of lava on the right.

Greg Vaughn

Waikoloa's Ocean 12th: three bunkers, ocean, lava and a two-tiered green!

Fairways on Waikoloa's King's Course include dramatic black lava outcroppings.

The 368-yard 8th hole is considered the best par 4 on the Beach Course. A large bunker sits in the center of the fairway 185 yards out. Bite off as much as you can chew -- either a short 140 yards or a 190 yards plus -- or you land in the bunker. The second shot should be to the right to miss the bunker and to land on the small green. Watch for this hole!

The most challenging hole is the 9th, a difficult 522-yard dogleg right. Three fairway bunkers are strategically placed at the dogleg, two on the approach and three guarding the green.

The most dramatic hole is the 12th, a 479-yard par 5. The fairway doglegs left and narrows on the approach to a two-tiered green protected by three bunkers. The view of ocean and black lava cliffs is breathtaking.

"The 18th is probably our best test," says Dennis Rose, Waikoloa's Director of Golf. The 18th's narrow fairway has a large bunker right, with palm trees and out-of-bounds on the left. At 374 yards, the hole plays into the wind to a long, hourglass-shaped green flanked by two bunkers.

Waikoloa added the King's Course in 1990. Designed by Tom Weiskopf and Jay Morrish, the King's is more challenging than the resort play of the Beach Course. It is longer -- 7,074 yards from the King's tees -- and features undulating fairways, large lava outcroppings, deep bunkers and a variety of greens, including one double green.

Weiskopf and Morrish are known for their driveable par 4s, and the 5th hole is the first to tempt you with a go-for-it attitude. With the prevailing wind at your back, the 327 yards could play considerably shorter.

To make the 5th more interesting, there are two large lava rocks on the left and a deep bunker on the right. However, it is still possible with a hint of a draw -- and a lucky bounce -- to achieve that ultimate dream: an eagle par 4.

The 6th hole, at 400 yards from the white tee, is the longest par 4 on the King's. The fairway is wide but the length is a challenge. The short hitter may be pitching for par and putting for bogey. The green is shared with the third hole, a condition unusual for Hawaii but typical of some Scottish courses.

The "Beauty and the Beast" hole is the 7th, a par 3. Your 155-yard drive must clear a perfectly positioned lake to land on a severely undulating green. Even a good shot to the green does not necessarily produce par here.

The 14th hole, a 601-yard par 5, is the longest on the course. Tradewinds usually work for you on this hole but if there's no wind, the green will be beyond reach even for long hitters. Aim the tee shot at a large lava boulder on the left and your second shot should be kept left of the deep fairway bunkers on the right. At this point, you still have 100 - 150 yards to a two-tier green. Birdies will be few on this hole!

The 15th, a par 3 measuring 139 yards from the blue tee, is similar to the front nine 7th. With a lake on the left and bunkers on the right, it demands accuracy with a mid-to-short iron. Par is a fine score on this hole.

Strong finishing holes are often the measure of a good golf course and in this department, the King's 18th is "awesome." The tee boxes are on a tiny peninsula protruding out onto a cliff. At 474 yards it is designed to be reachable in two but with a narrowing fairway and a dropoff to the ocean on the left, it might be better to lay up to the right of the green. This hole sees birdies -- but many more bogies!

Overall, the greatest challenge on the King's Course is handling the holes that face into the wind. If you hit high, you lose yardage. If you adjust your stroke and keep it down, the fierce undulations of the fairways will stop you dead. The answer can only be to play the wind carefully, and "medium high."

As a complement to the more forgiving Beach Course, the King's Course is perfect. The two add up to great golf and are major contributors to the Big Island's growing reputation as a premier golf destination.

Both golf courses have large clubhouses with restaurants, pro shops and other amenities of a first-class resort. The Beach Course is also home to the Waikoloa Golf Academy.

Director of Golf:
Dennis Rose

For further information:
Waikoloa Golf Club
HCO2 Box 5575
Waikoloa, Hawaii, HI 96743
(808) 885-4647

DISCOVERY HARBOR

Opened in 1971, Discovery Harbor is yet another creation of renowned golf course architect Robert Trent Jones, Sr. Every hole was designed to take advantage of both ocean and mountain views.

This remote and wondrous setting for the southernmost golf course in the U.S. attracts more than just golfers. Over 1,000 condominiums surround the links.

The course was originally free but with new Japanese ownership since 1985, there are nominal playing fees ($13.00 green fee; $12.00 club fee). There is still no charge at the driving range.

Discovery Harbor has a limited service pro shop that rents clubs but does not repair them. The dress code here is very liberal, golf shoes being the only requirement. Golf carts are mandatory.

Despite only 10 widely scattered bunkers and no water hazards, this is still a difficult par 72 course of 6,640 yards. Right off, the 420-yard par 4 first hole proves a tough challenge. You will need a long and accurate drive to give you a decent approach shot on this one.

Recently, the course has undergone improvements to the tees and greens of the back nine.

Except for the high season which begins in November, reservations are not required for Monday through Friday play. Reservations are necessary on weekends.

Resort guests have access to the tennis courts. There is a convenient clubhouse where you can relax, have a drink and escape the "vog" (volcanic smog) that occasionally drifts over from where Kilauea's lava flows into the sea.

General Manager:
Katsuhiko Ando

For further information:
Discovery Harbor Golf
 & Country Club
Kahiki St., Hawaii, HI 96722
(808) 929-7353

The 330-yard par 4 tenth hole gets longer when the wind is up.

Vogelsberger

WAIKOLOA VILLAGE GOLF COURSE

Designed by Robert Trent Jones, Jr. and opened in 1972, Waikoloa is a well-manicured 6,791-yard, par 72 course with plenty of challenges. Typical of the Jones style, it has well-placed fairway bunkers, nine doglegs and two lakes. The fairways are bordered by palms, Norfolk pines, kiawe, ironwood and eucalyptus trees.

The number one handicap hole is the 5th. Measuring 382 yards from the regular tee, the narrow fairway leads up to a green surrounded by four bunkers. Playing into the wind causes this hole to play much longer than it measures. Careful club selection is a must.

The par 3 third hole is 171 yards from an elevated tee. The winds blow right to left and can reach considerable velocity. To the left is a lake and the break is also to the left. The green is undulating.

The 9th hole is one of four par 5's. Measuring 495 yards, it is a pleasant way to finish the first nine and an easy par.

The back nine starts with a 330-yard par 4 that doglegs left. A bunker blocks the short route and another bunker on the long side awaits your mishit. The approach shot must take into account two more bunkers flanking the green.

The 18th is a fine hole to finish on. It is a 490-yard dogleg left with two fairway bunkers waiting for your first shot. The entrance to the green is completely surrounded by water that is about 80 yards wide. You have to think this hole out well before you play it.

Among the amenities at the clubhouse are a restaurant, snack bar, cocktail lounge, tennis court, driving range, putting green and a full service pro shop.

Head Professional:
Charles Rogosheske, PGA

For further information:
Waikoloa Village Golf Club
P.O. Box 383910
Waikoloa, Hawaii, HI 96738
(808) 883-9621

Playing golf on the summit of the world's most active volcano can be a moving experience!

VOLCANO GOLF AND COUNTRY CLUB

Over 4,000 feet above sea level, the Volcano Golf and Country Club is set on the slopes of Mauna Loa near the Kilauea crater, the world's most active volcano. The course is nestled amid red-blossomed ohia trees on the Volcanoes National Park grounds.

It is often chilly and damp up here but the fairways and tees of stiff Kikuya grass give you a great lie. On the other hand, should you land in the rough, you will understand why it is so called. So stay on the fairway. Use a club or two less than normal here as the altitude adds distance to your shots.

The fairways roll gently while the greens are fast and small. Both are quite straightforward. It is safe to advise, "when in doubt, putt straight."

The original Volcano Golf and Country Club was built in 1922 by a group of Scots. In 1967 it was redesigned by Arthur Jack Snyder who expanded it to 18 holes. Then in 1983, Bill Hiyashi remodeled the course again, adding 4 ponds and 30 bunkers to the 5,800-yard, par 72 layout.

If you think two bunkers and a water hazard make the 180-yard, par 3 sixth hole tough, wait till you get to the fifteenth! It is a long par 4 past eucalyptus trees with a dog-leg left, hitting into the wind onto an elevated green.

The course is open to the public 7 days a week and allows sixsomes during slow times. Golf carts are mandatory as are golf shoes and shirts. Dress is casual.

There is a full service pro shop, driving range and restaurant that serves cocktails.

Director of Golf:
  Dante Estrada

For further information:
Volcano Golf and Country Club
P. O. Box 46
Volcanoes National Park,
HI 96718
(808) 967-7331

SeaMountain at Punalu'u Resort

SeaMountain Golf Course at the Punalu'u Resort is a charming place to visit, stay and play or merely relax. It is situated just above the shores of Punalu'u's famous black sand beaches, between the flanks of the majestic Mauna Loa volcano and the pounding Pacific, hence the name "SeaMountain." You can imagine the views.

The course was designed by Arthur Jack Snyder and opened in 1971. SeaMountain's 6,106-yard, par 72 layout features 5 ponds, 22 sand bunkers and countless lava formations. In fact, there is a mass of the hard black stuff sitting right on the 6th fairway. And that is no more fun than the 15-foot gully that bisects the 14th, a 135-yard, par 3 hole.

The most challenging holes here, however, are the 15th and 17th. The former is a downhill par 5 with a creek and monkey pod trees running along the right. The 17th is dotted with monkey pods as well and has 3 lakes waiting for your ball on the left side of the fairway.

There are no restrictions on guest policy but appropriate golf wear is required. Golf carts are mandatory. There is a full service pro shop and driving range on the premises.

Resort accommodations include 76 luxury condos with swimming pool, tennis courts (free to golf guests), the Aspen Institute conference facilities and the Punalu'u Village Restaurant. And of course there are the black sand beaches, hiking and horseback riding for nature lovers.

Director of Golf:
Rip Collins

For further information:
SeaMountain
   at Punalu'u Resort
P.O. Box 85
Pahala, Hawaii, HI 96777
(808) 928-6222

HILO MUNICIPAL GOLF COURSE

Hilo Municipal Golf Course opened in 1951 and is the Big Island's only municipal course. Designed by Willard G. Wilkinson, this 18-hole course was built on land that formerly belonged to the Waiakea Sugar Plantation. It now measures 6,006 yards from the white tees and is a par 72.

The Hilo Municipal Golf Course is a great favorite of local Hilo players. Trees of every variety line the fairways. There are hibiscus, monkey pod, banyan, eucalyptus and a variety of palms. Located as it is on the windward side of the island, expect play to be occasionally interrupted by life-giving rain, which in turn creates a lush and green course that is sometimes slow with excess water. There are no sand bunkers and many of the greens are elevated.

Facilities include a putting green, clubhouse, restaurant, cocktail lounge and snack bar. Reservations are necessary as 90,000 rounds are played each year.

Golf Professional:
Rodney Acia

For further information:
Hilo Municipal Golf Course
340 Haihai St.
Hilo, HI 96720
(808) 959-7711

HAMAKUA COUNTRY CLUB

Hamakua Country Club opened in 1926. Built by plantation workers on 19 acres of very hilly terrain, it lies north of Hilo near the town of Honoka'a. The rolling, narrow, tree-lined fairways and small greens make this par 66 a hard one to break. The 9th hole layout is composed of six par 4's and three par 3's. Fairways cross one another on no less than six holes. Courtesy and caution are in order here. The USGA rating is 63.2 with a 109.2 slope rating.

There are the usual bunkers and a few water hazards (sometimes waterless depending on the rain) over the 5,000-yard course.

Hamakua Country Club hosts the Annual Macadamia Nut Masters Golf Tournament every August. They use Macadamia nuts instead of balls. Contestants say mac nuts really "ping" and are very strong!

Guests are welcome any time except during tournament play. Dress is casual. Hamakua has no carts or restaurant. However, cocktails are available in the small clubhouse.

When you arrive at Hamakua, you are greeted by an "honor box" and a sign that states: "$10 to play 1 hole; $10 for 9 holes; $10 for 18 holes; $10 all day."

For further information:
Hamakua Country Club
P.O. Box 751
Honoka'a, Hawaii, HI 96727
(808) 775-7244

The annual Macadamia Nut Masters is played on Hamakua's straight-ahead fairways.

NANILOA COUNTRY CLUB

Naniloa is a 9-hole city course spread over 65 acres of land circumscribed by Hilo's picturesque Banyan Drive. Nearby are a quaint Japanese garden and a footbridge that takes you out to a small park on Coconut Island in Hilo Bay.

The 5,610-yard, par 70 layout was designed by Tommy Ukauka and opened in 1968. It is a predominantly flat course with no bunkers but lots of banyan trees.

The 200-yard 8th hole is a challenging par 3 with large mango trees to the left, out-of-bounds on the right, and a two-level green in front.

The 395-yard 9th hole is a par 4, with a dogleg left off the tee. Both sides of this fairway are out-of-bounds. You will need a long second shot here to reach the green.

For the dedicated, there is a driving range open at night at Naniloa. Golf attire (including shoes) is required while golf carts are available but not mandatory. There are no hand carts.

Just across Banyan Street is the Hawaii Naniloa Hotel with a pool, tennis courts, spa and even yachts to utilize.

Guests are always welcome. Keep in mind, however, that Hilo catches a lot of rain, averaging 150 inches per year.

For further information:
Naniloa Country Club
120 Banyan Drive
Hilo, HI 96720
(808) 935-3000

GOLF USA
big island's one stop golf shop
KONA GOLF SHOP, INC

▶ **FEATURING:**
Indoor Range
Sportech Swing Analyzer Computer
(Endorsed by the P.G.A. Tour)
Computer Fittings

▶ **EVERYDAY LOW PRICES ON:**
Name Brand Clubs
Clothing and Shoes
Gifts and Accessories
329-2292
Centrally located in Kona in Kaiwi Square on the corner of Highway 19 and Kaiwi Street.
"Over 60 Stores Nationwide"

MasterCard VISA AMERICAN EXPRESS

74-5565 Luhia St.   Kailua-Kona, HI 96740

Francis H. I'i Brown Golf Courses

The Francis H. I'i Brown Courses at the Mauna Lani Resort are a delight to behold for any golfing aficionado. Situated on the sunny Kohala Coast, the resort and courses are built atop a lava flow right at the ocean's edge, a remarkable coupling of nature and man.

The courses are literally carved out of jagged lava flows. Thousands of tons of soil were trucked in from other parts of the island. The result is two imposing courses on a sometimes bleak-looking moonscape.

In the early days, the area was known by the Hawaiian name of the fish ponds, Kalahuipua'a. These royal fish ponds, which are the basis for several Hawaiian legends, meander close to the ocean shore and are still part of the South Course.

The surrounding scenery at Mauna Lani adds much to the enjoyment of playing, and the landscaping of the courses is a visual pleasure. The green velvet Tifton fairways and Tifdwarf greens are as well manicured as any resort you can play. These courses are so striking that when you first see them, the only shooting you will want to do is with a camera!

Mauna Lani is also a great place to lose balls. When your ball goes out-of-bounds and into the lava, it will bounce about a dozen times before settling into some deep, dark crevice.

The golf complex is named after Francis H. I'i Brown, who was reputed to be a great golfer, a superb storyteller and a hardy drinker. At one point, Brown was concurrently the amateur champion of Hawaii, California and Japan.

During the 1964 Olympics, Brown met and played a round of golf with Noboru Gotoh, a businessman who had built his Tokyu Corporation from a tiny railroad company to a huge Japanese colossus. From that meeting came an enduring friendship and a new golf course -- the Mauna Lani.

The original Francis H. I'i Brown course was designed by Homer Flint and Raymond Cain as a par 72 eighteen, measuring 6,370 from the men's tees.

In 1991, new holes were added and a team of Flint plus Robin Nelson and Rodney Wright re-designed the course into two new eighteens, the North Course and

Mauna Lani's courses are a study in contrasts of color, texture and character.

the South Course. The two courses differ in character largely because they are situated on lava flows of different geological age.

The South Course is built on the geologically younger Kaniku lava flow and offers golf on a moonscape. The par 72 course measures 6,370 yards from the white tees.

The 4th hole is the first true challenge of the South, a 564-yard par 5. To make the green in regulation you'll have to avoid water, lava and sand flanking a fairway that doglegs slightly right and funnels to a long narrow green. The green slopes back to front and is guarded by water to the left, sand and lava to the right and mounds at the back. This long hole will test both your endurance and skill.

The South 7th is a doozy of a par 3. It requires a long downhill carry -- over 200 yards from the blues -- of shoreline lava cliffs to reach a two-tiered green whose surface ripples like the ocean. And that's just where your ball will lie if you misjudge the on-shore winds and mishit left! Framed by ocean on the left, a windswept kiawe grove behind and salt-and-pepper sand dunes to the right, the 7th is one you're sure to remember.

The South 15th hole has been famous for over a decade as the signature 6th hole of the original course. This par 3 ranges from 132 to 199 yards from tees that rise from the lava like elevated green tables. The tee shot is over a sea that can be calm as a lake or whipped wild by huge surf, made all the more exciting by gusty crosswinds. If you are a member of the hackers club, this hole can be a ball-eater. The green is fairly flat but is guarded by five bunkers. During winter months, you have the additional distraction of whale activity on the ocean.

The North Course is a par 72 measuring 6,335 yards from the white tees and is built on a brownish-colored lava bed much older than that of the South. The North is characterized by rolling terrain and kiawe forests, with trees very much a factor in play. A 230-acre archaeological district lies on the course's northern boundary.

The 3rd hole is a good example of what the North has to offer. A par 4 dogleg left, your drive must contend with trees lining both sides of a narrow fairway and several trees in the fairway itself. Avoid the in-fairway kiawe tree on your drive and you risk a bunker on the right. The green is guarded by bunkers left and right.

The 15th hole is one of the hardest holes to handle. This 471-yard par 5 is a severe dogleg right. A big hitter may cut the trees at the dogleg's elbow with a carry of some 230 yards, but target areas are spotted with bunkers. After the dogleg the fairway runs downhill. To reach the green, you must shoot straight as an arrow between bunkers on the left and water on the right. The green itself is guarded by three more bunkers.

Mauna Lani is a rare pleasure. The golf courses are challenging and the resort is unsurpassable. No wonder Golf Magazine has presented Mauna Lani a Gold Award as one of the top golf resorts in America -- and has done so three times in a row!

Mauna Lani is also the site of the annual Senior Skins Game, one of golf's most popular televised events. Arnold Palmer has won three times, Jack Nicklaus once. The Skins Game is held in January of each year.

Head Professional:
  Scott Bridges

For further information:
Francis H. I'i Brown Golf Course
P.O. Box 4959
Kohala Coast, Hawaii, HI 96743
(808) 885-6655

ALOHA KAUAI

Known also as "The Garden Isle" because of its rich vegetation, Kauai is also the oldest, and according to many, the most beautiful island in the Hawaiian chain.

There is much to see and do on Kauai—a canoe ride along the magnificent NaPali Coast; a helicopter flight to see incredible waterfalls cascading hundreds of feet to green moss-covered cliffs; a drive to the "Grand Canyon of the Pacific", Waimea Canyon and the Kalalau lookout; deep sea fishing, water skiing, kayaking or a trip up the Wailua River to a verdant fern grotto.

Kauai's golf courses weathered 1992's Hurricane Iniki quite well—in fact, they were virtually unscathed. The island vegetation has bounced back nicely, restoring the landscape to its original lush, green beauty.

Kauai has an unusually large number of top-ranked courses. Among your choices for championship golf are three—the Prince, Makai and Kiele courses—that rank in the Top 100 Golf Courses in America. The Prince Course and Makai Courses, both designed by Robert Trent Jones, Jr., offer excellent play at Princeville Resort, near Hanalei on the island's north shore. The Kiele Course at Kauai Lagoons Golf & Racquet Club is a Jack Nicklaus design spread along a magnificent oceanside setting in the Lihue area.

Other award-winners are the Poipu Bay Resort Golf Course and the Lagoons Course at Kauai Lagoons, which are ranked in the Top 100 Resort Courses in the nation. Poipu Bay Resort Golf Course was awarded the honor of having the nationally televised PGA Shootout held there in 1994. Kauai's municipal course, Wailua, is ranked among the top 25 Municipal Courses in the U.S. And in a state noted for its golf, the Prince Course at Princeville is ranked "Best Golf Course in Hawaii" by Golf Digest and in the top 10 in the U.S.

There are many reasons to travel to Kauai, but when it comes to the golfer the question simply becomes one of timing—not if you should go but when!

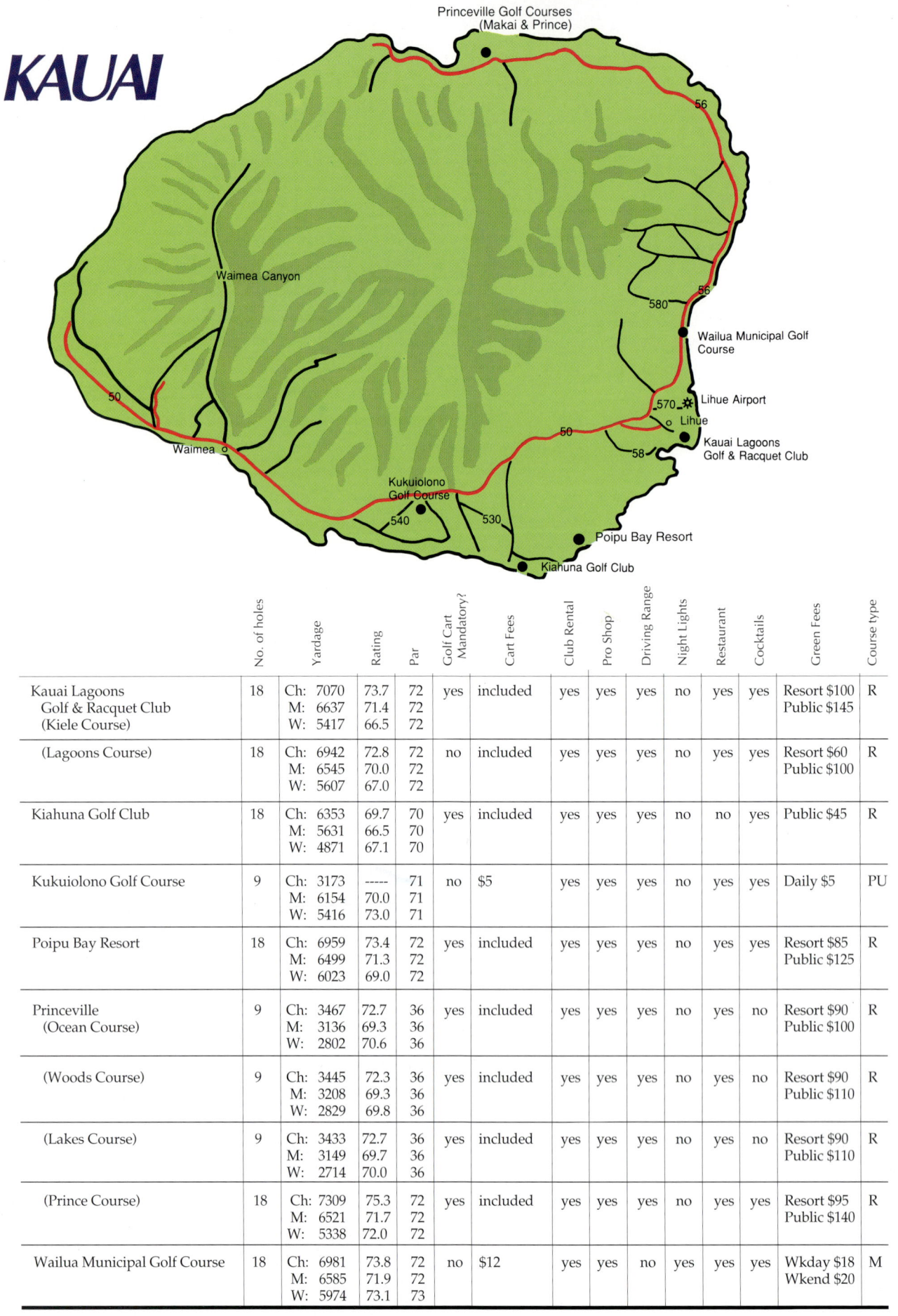

KAUAI

	No. of holes	Yardage	Rating	Par	Golf Cart Mandatory?	Cart Fees	Club Rental	Pro Shop	Driving Range	Night Lights	Restaurant	Cocktails	Green Fees	Course type
Kauai Lagoons Golf & Racquet Club (Kiele Course)	18	Ch: 7070 M: 6637 W: 5417	73.7 71.4 66.5	72 72 72	yes	included	yes	yes	yes	no	yes	yes	Resort $100 Public $145	R
(Lagoons Course)	18	Ch: 6942 M: 6545 W: 5607	72.8 70.0 67.0	72 72 72	no	included	yes	yes	yes	no	yes	yes	Resort $60 Public $100	R
Kiahuna Golf Club	18	Ch: 6353 M: 5631 W: 4871	69.7 66.5 67.1	70 70 70	yes	included	yes	yes	yes	no	no	yes	Public $45	R
Kukuiolono Golf Course	9	Ch: 3173 M: 6154 W: 5416	----- 70.0 73.0	71 71 71	no	$5	yes	yes	yes	no	yes	yes	Daily $5	PU
Poipu Bay Resort	18	Ch: 6959 M: 6499 W: 6023	73.4 71.3 69.0	72 72 72	yes	included	yes	yes	yes	no	yes	yes	Resort $85 Public $125	R
Princeville (Ocean Course)	9	Ch: 3467 M: 3136 W: 2802	72.7 69.3 70.6	36 36 36	yes	included	yes	yes	yes	no	yes	no	Resort $90 Public $100	R
(Woods Course)	9	Ch: 3445 M: 3208 W: 2829	72.3 69.3 69.8	36 36 36	yes	included	yes	yes	yes	no	yes	no	Resort $90 Public $110	R
(Lakes Course)	9	Ch: 3433 M: 3149 W: 2714	72.7 69.7 70.0	36 36 36	yes	included	yes	yes	yes	no	yes	no	Resort $90 Public $110	R
(Prince Course)	18	Ch: 7309 M: 6521 W: 5338	75.3 71.7 72.0	72 72 72	yes	included	yes	yes	yes	no	yes	yes	Resort $95 Public $140	R
Wailua Municipal Golf Course	18	Ch: 6981 M: 6585 W: 5974	73.8 71.9 73.1	72 72 73	no	$12	yes	yes	no	yes	yes	yes	Wkday $18 Wkend $20	M

R = Resort   PR = Private
PU = Public   M = Municipal
ALL RATES SUBJECT TO CHANGE

Site of The 1994 PGA Grand Slam of Golf.

A classic location for a classic event. Spectators at this year's PGA Grand Slam of Golf faced a tough decision — watching the play or marvelling at the scenery! The million dollar sports highlight with its $400,000 first prize, attracted the world's finest golfers and was held at one of the most breathtaking spots on the face of the earth. The Poipu Bay Resort Golf Course on the garden island of Kauai, designed by Robert Trent Jones II, with a lot of help from Mother Nature, is one of Hawaii's top-ranked golf courses. Come to play the championship 18-hole course or just to rediscover how beautiful life is . . . in Paradise.

Poipu Bay Resort
GOLF COURSE

*2250 Ainako Street
Koloa, Kauai, HI 96756
Phone (808) 742-8711
Toll Free 1-800-858-6300
Hawaiian Time
6:30am - 6:30pm*

The scenery at the Prince Course at Princeville is out of this world -- as are some of the scores on one of Hawaii's toughest courses!

Princeville

Hanalei Bay on the North Shore of the Island of Kauai has long been regarded as one of the most beautiful places in the world. Since Hollywood discovered the natural beauty of the island, its magnificent primitive splendor has enchanted millions around the world in more than thirty major movie productions, including *South Pacific*, *Raiders of the Lost Ark*, *Indiana Jones and the Temple of Doom*, *Uncommon Valor*, and *Blue Hawaii*.

Today, Hanalei is attracting not only moviemakers but shotmakers as well, as golfers from around the world discover the extraordinary Makai and Prince golf courses of Princeville.

"In all the world," said Robert Trent Jones Jr., Princeville's architect, "I never expected to find a more spectacularly beautiful place to build a golf course than Princeville, overlooking Hanalei Bay." Lush verdant valleys, cascading waterfalls, rolling hills, windswept beaches, rainforest and tropical fauna of all colors have been integrated into Jones' incredible vision of what the game of golf was meant to be.

The first course Jones completed at Princeville was the Makai Course, which has been rated among "America's 100 Greatest Golf Courses" by Golf Digest magazine for 16 consecutive years, the only course in Hawaii so honored. The Makai course was also listed in USA Today's Top 100 Courses in the United States and is presently on Golf Digest's Top 25 Resort Courses.

The Makai Course offers three nines, each a par 36 --the 3,433-yard Lakes, the 3,445-yard Woods and the 3,467-yard Ocean -- which extend like spokes from the clubhouse. Each has its own distinctive character and scenic flavor as reflected in the names, and any combination of the three provides an enjoyable and challenging round of golf.

The Ocean nine winds its way to the high cliffs overlooking Hanalei Bay where waves crash against black rocks and beaches. The 7th hole, spectacular and intimidating, is a great test of nerve and skill. A 204-yard par 3 from the championship tees, the tee shot to the green must carry over both the Pacific Ocean and a dense tropical jungle that plunges 150 feet. Updrafts can do strange things to a golf ball, so careful attention must be given to wind conditions and club selection.

The Woods nine meanders through forest and undergrowth towards the mountains. Most agree that the 6th hole, a 447-yard par 4 that doglegs to the right, is the most challenging. From the tee, it's tempting to try cutting the dogleg to avoid the out-of-bounds on the left side of the fairway. However, beware of a large fairway bunker some 200 yards down the fairway on the right that waits for anyone seeking a shorter way to the green. Even with a good drive, a wood or long iron will be needed to reach the well-bunkered green in regulation.

On the Lake nine, the 439-yard 8th hole is a gut check. With large trees guarding the right, the tee shot must be hit long and left center of the fairway for the best approach shot to the green. On the second shot, accuracy is critical as the fairway suddenly narrows to a green that is protected by a large lake on the right front and along the entire right side. Aiming too far left, however, brings into play two large greenside bunkers positioned above the hole facing the water. Making par on this hole demands nothing less than two great golf shots.

The 27-hole Makai Course has its own facilities, from driving range and putting green to a full-service pro shop and the Makai snack bar.

Of the more than 150 courses Robert Trent Jones, Jr. has designed or redesigned in over 20 countries, he has called the Prince "one of the top five courses I've ever designed." He used all the diverse elements of the terrain to develop each hole's character, then subtly blended intrigue and excitement into their design.

Since opening for play in 1990, the awesome combination of Hanalei and Jones' imagination has resulted in numerous awards and accolades. Golf Digest named the Prince the "Best New Resort Golf Course in the United States" and the "Best Golf Course in Hawaii." Golf Magazine ranked the Prince as one of the "Top 10 New Courses to Play" and among the "100 Greatest Golf Courses in the United States."

The 7,309-yard par 72 Prince Course is laid out across 390 acres of rolling tableland overlooking the Pacific Ocean and bisected by deep ravines, tropical jungles, natural streams and waterfalls.

There is a genuine sense of adventure when playing the Prince. The character of each hole is challenging to the extreme. Case in point is the 7th hole, a par 3 known as "Da Pali." This hole is reminiscent of the famous 16th at Cypress Point, but reversed with the lay up area on the right and the ocean on the left. With multiple tee boxes, the hole ranges from 205 yards in length with a 180-yard carry against the wind, to a more relaxing 98 yards from the women's tee to the green on a cliffside where waves can be seen breaking on the reef off Anini Beach.

The 13th hole, known as the "Waterfall," is as difficult as it is beautiful. A dogleg right 418-yard par 4, this hole requires a long iron or fairway wood for the tee shot. The target fairway is cut through tropical jungle to a landing area 200 yards away where it doglegs right. The green is tucked away against a grotto with a cascading waterfall that gives the entire scene a serene and peaceful ambience. Definitely a distraction, but worth every bit of it.

The Prince Golf and Country Club is situated on a rise overlooking the course. The 60,000 square foot clubhouse has panoramic views sweeping from Mount Namalakoma on the left to Bali Hai in the distance and across the broad blue expanse of the Pacific to the horizon. The clubhouse offers a restaurant and lounge, a health and beauty spa, function and teaching rooms, locker rooms and one of the most modern pro shop facilities.

Other facilities include a 1,200 square foot putting green, another 1,200 square foot chipping area offering every situation one would care to practice and a driving range with three separate teeing locations to four greens below. The Prince Restaurant, open for breakfast, lunch and dinner, has a broad selection of American and Japanese fare.

Director of Golf:
Bob Higgins

For further information:
Princeville Golf Course
P.O. Box 3040
Princeville, Kauai, HI 96722
(808) 826-3580 -- Makai Course
(808) 826-5000 -- Prince Course

Ancient Hawaiian rock walls and bright bougainvillea surround Kiahuna's first green.

KIAHUNA GOLF CLUB

Opened in 1984, the Kiahuna Golf Club at Poipu Beach is a championship course on Kauai's sunny south shore. The weather is ideal. The rolling fairways and undulating well-trapped greens are just a few minutes from well-known hotels and resorts such as the Sheraton Kauai, the Waiohai Hotel and the Kiahuna Plantation Resort. Kiahuna is owned by the Sports Shinko Group of Japan.

The course is built on an ancient Hawaiian village site and the layout preserves several archaeological areas. There are five major sites including lava tubes, irrigation aqueducts and the remains of a house believed to have been constructed in the early 1800's.

Designed by world famous golf architect, Robert Trent Jones, Jr., the course is nearly 6,400 yards long, par 70 with plenty of water hazards including two holes played over Waikomo Stream. Jones' rolling mound configurations leave little opportunity for flat lies and he says the course reminds him of some of the famous courses in Scotland.

Kiahuna requires good club selection and careful consideration of the wind factor, which as often as not is a crosswind starting halfway down the fairway. Hazards crop up in unexpected places -- you find bunkers just waiting for you to mishit.

If you can drive past the bunkers or more typically right up to them, you will have an enjoyable game. If not, it will be a long day!

The 15th hole is a long par 4 with a dramatic setting and a well bunkered, kidney-shaped green that is tough to putt. The third hole is a long par 3 playing into a right-to-left crosswind to a double-level green fronted by a stream of varying widths and depths. The tendency here is to underclub.

For further information:
Kiahuna Golf Club
Kiahuna Plantation Road
Koloa, Kauai, HI 96756
(808) 742-9595

KAUAI LAGOONS GOLF & RACQUET CLUB

Aerial view of the spectacular 16th hole of the Lagoons Course.

Kauai Lagoons Golf & Racquet Club includes two 18-hole golf courses, spa and tennis courts surrounded by 40 acres of man-made lagoons overlooking the Pacific Ocean.

Since its opening in 1988, Kauai Lagoons has reaped acclaim as one of the best American resort courses by both Golf Magazine and Golf Digest. Kauai Lagoon's oceanside setting provides both high and low handicappers challenging play and spectacular scenery for a game of golf.

"I was asked to create one of the great golf courses of the world," said designer Jack Nicklaus, who also serves as Director of Golf. "The site is probably one of the most magnificent pieces of property I have ever seen. It gave us the tremendous opportunity to create something memorable for Hawaii."

The Kiele Course is named after resort developer Chris Hemmeter's daughter. "Kiele" is loosely translated as "the sweet smelling fragrance of the gardenia flower." From the gold tee, the 7,100 yard, par 72 layout is recommended for golfers with handicaps of 20 or less. Four sets of tees, however, offer an array of shotmaking possibilities. No matter where you tee up, Kiele is still a demanding test of skill and daring.

For example, the dramatic 519-yard 6th hole is very unforgiving. A par 5, your tee shot must carry a deep and lush tropical ravine. Your second shot requires touch and concentration to miss a large fairway bunker on the right.

The 169-yard 8th is a par 3, downhill to a tight green bordered by a pond on the right, complete with swans. Wind can make or break you on this hole. With trades blowing left to right, the pond comes into play, and with a bunker left front, a forward position on the pin can make your options seem limited. Visually stunning and intimidating, this is a par 3 that is nice to make.

Another test of nerves is the picturesque 330-yard 16th, a par 4 which slopes downhill toward the sea. The short yardage is deceiving as this hole requires finesse, skill and a pinball-style bank shot to reach the green. The small green is built on a lava ledge alongside the ocean, so a shot aimed directly at the flag can roll off into the sea. The right way to play the hole is to aim for the base of the hill on the right and allow the ball to pitch off the slope and roll onto the green.

Kiele's finishing hole is a long, 431-yard par 4 occasionally made longer by swirling trade winds. The fairway borders a lake along its entire length on the right and your second or sometimes third shot is made to a small island green surrounded on three sides by water.

With its elaborate bunkering, bold terracing and cliffhanger greensites laid out over 262 acres of one of the most beautiful seaside properties to be found in Hawaii, the Kiele Course can be expected to host a major professional tournament sometime in the future.

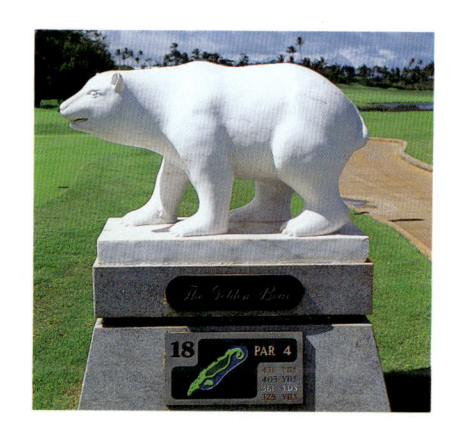

The Lagoons Course, also designed by Nicklaus, opened for play in 1989. Designed as a complement to the more demanding Kiele Course, the 6,942-yard par 72 Lagoons is a links-style course ideally suited to recreational golf. The course wraps around a 40-acre network of lagoon waterways and a menagerie of exotic wildlife. As your play progresses along 10 miles of lagoon shoreline, you can glimpse flamingos, wallabies, monkeys, cranes and macaws which inhabit seven island wildlife

91

sanctuaries.

Although designed to be a pleasant challenge and not a pitched battle, the Lagoons Course should not be underestimated. Trade winds often raise the difficulty factor on the Lagoons Course several notches.

For example, on both the 414-yard, par 4 first hole and the 426-yard, par 4 second hole, tee and fairway shots are dead into the wind to tight fairways.

On the back nine, if you have a tendency to hook shots, expect problems on the 449-yard 14th hole, a par 4 with a lake on the left. The 18th hole is another gut wrencher, as approach shots must be hit close to the pin. Then, every bit of touch and skill will be required to two putt on this fast, undulating, four-tiered green.

A nice perk is that all guests playing at Kauai Lagoons are made temporary members of the Golf & Racquet Club. Green fees include unlimited practice balls, shoe and club cleaning, a roomy locker and admission to the spa.

Kauai Lagoons Golf & Racquet Club includes a pleasant, open-air restaurant, The Terrace, open for lunch daily. An on course snack shop offers juice, soda, coffee, sandwiches and the like all day. Tennis is also available on eight plexipaved courts.

Head Professional:
Ron Rawls, PGA

For further information:
Kauai Lagoons Resort
P.O. Box 3330
Kalapaki Beach, HI 96766
(808) 241-6000

Your tee shot must clear this deep jungle covered ravine.

Poipu Bay's 15th is a 401-yard par 4 that plays with the wind -- and between the bunkers!

Poipu Bay Resort Golf Course

Home of the PGA Grand Slam of Golf

With the opening of the Poipu Bay Golf Resort, Kauai has added a new name to its already impressive roster of premium resort golf courses. Designed by Robert Trent Jones, Jr., the links-style course is long and rugged with over 6,900 yards of rolling fairways from the gold tees, large undulating greens, four lakes, and more than 80 strategically placed fairway and greenside bunkers. Built along the cliffs of Keoneloa Bay adjacent to the Hyatt Regency Kauai, Jones described the new eighteen-hole resort golf course as the "Pebble Beach of the South Pacific."

The setting for the course is striking. Jones was particularly careful to preserve ancient Hawaiian archaeological sites such as heiaus (temples), which can be found throughout the golf course. There are incredible views of Mount Haupu, the beach and ocean cliffs. Pods of humpback whales can be seen passing by off-

The dramatic cliffs of Keoneloa Bay at Poipu Bay Resort Golf Course

shore during the winter months.

Under windy conditions, the course is a true test of skill and stamina. With four sets of tees from which to choose -- gold, blue, white and red -- golfers have the chance to challenge the course at the best of their skill level.

That challenge begins at the 2nd hole, a 482-yard par 5 dead into the wind on most days. From the tee the drive is hit over a rise to a fairway that doglegs right. You may be tempted to try to cut the dogleg but trouble awaits in the form of a bunker, hidden behind the rise. When the wind is up, this hole plays very long. Even strong hitters will need at least two woods and a long iron to make par.

The ninth hole is another test of grit. From the blue tees, this par 4 measures only 367 yards. However, miss the fairway left or right and you're in one of the deep bunkers on either side. Beware also of the ancient Hawaiian heiau on the right side, just beyond the bunker. Mess with Hawaiian gods and it will cost you a penalty stroke to drop!

On the back nine, the par 3, 166-yard 11th hole separates the lion-hearted from the meek. The tee shot is from an elevated tee to a green guarded by a large lake on the right front and the entire right side. Any attempt to play it safe by hitting it left will bring into play a large bunker. The key to par on this hole is club selection. When hitting into swirling trade winds, it may take a wood to hit the green in one. If you make par on this hole, congratulate yourself, you will have earned it.

The 16th hole, at 472 yards, is a spectacular par 4 reminiscent of the great finishing hole at Pebble Beach. Hitting the green in regulation on this long hole is very demanding. The entire left side of the fairway borders the ocean and beach where green sea turtles and the endangered monk seal sometimes frolic. The only safe way to the green is playing with extreme caution the right side of the fairway on the approach shot, avoiding greenside bunkers all along the right. Also, check if the pin is placed on the front part of the green. If it is, try to place your approach shot below the flag. Putting from above the hole will require a treacherous downhill putt on this undulating green.

The second par 3 on the back nine is one of the most visually striking holes on the course. The elevated 17th tee is set on an ancient Hawaiian stone formation overlooking a gully with trees, dense foliage and thick bushes. The green, protected by a large bunker in front and on the left side, is 199 yards from the blue tees but club up if the wind is in your face. Before you hit your tee shot, however, take a moment to appreciate the incredible ocean scenery of the Poipu coast.

The Poipu Bay Golf Resort is one of those courses that seems to play differently no matter how many times you play. Every round of golf means new challenges and you'll find yourself cleaning every club in your bag at the end of the round.

Practice facilities at the Poipu Bay Resort Golf Course include a 10-acre driving range, 12,000 square feet of putting greens, and practice bunkers with the teaching facility just adjacent to the driving range.

The 21,000 square foot clubhouse, overlooking a crystal clear lake and the 18th green, is one of the most modern facilities of its kind. The pro shop is tastefully laid out and offers the best names in golf equipment and accessories. At the clubhouse restaurant, the Poipu Bay Bar and Grill, guests can enjoy breakfast, lunch or dinner while admiring the captivating views.

Director of Golf:
Ron Kiaaina

For futher information:
Poipu Bay Resort
Golf Course
2250 Ainako Street
Koloa, Kauai, HI 96756
(808) 742-9489

WAILUA GOLF COURSE

The most beautiful municipal golf course in Hawaii is on Kauai. The Wailua Golf Course was recognized by <u>Golf</u> <u>Digest</u> in 1981 as one of the 10 best municipals in the country.

Located 10 miles north of Lihue on Kauai's southeast coast and surrounded by major resorts, Wailua is skirted by the magnificent Kalepa ridge to the west and white sand beaches and blue Pacific Ocean to the east. The Kauai topography in general is among the most awe inspiring in the world and Wailua is no exception.

Four greens are right on the ocean where the views are breathtaking and tropical foliage abounds. Developed slowly and without the benefit of an architect (an attribute it shares with such mainland courses as Oakmont and Pebble Beach), Wailua's first nine was started in 1920 as a six hole course. Francis I'i Brown, famous for his Big Island development of Mauna Lani, upgraded it to a nine. From then, the history belongs to Toyo Shirai, a humble, hard-working giver of time and energy, who after more than 3 years won approval from the state for the second nine.

Wailua's 3 par 14th requires a long carry over a deep swale to a small green.

The greens are small and medium speed. The challenge comes in getting there via narrow fairways. The 16th hole is a typical example. From the regular tee it is a 346-yard par 4 which doglegs left. The undulating fairway slopes to the right.

The 2nd hole runs adjacent to the beach where the pounding surf and spray can easily affect your concentration. The wind blows onshore and is from left to right at about 15 mph. It is 441 yards from the regular tee and earns a one handicap.

Another interesting hole is the 7th. Smack in front of the green is a huge bunker. Together with the green it re-

Overshoot the 17th at Wailua and it's water; undershoot and it's sand!

Palm trees and towering Norfolk pines frame Kukuiolono's fast-running greens.

sembles a smiling face. And you can smile too, for the chances are high that you land right there!

Overall, Wailua is your perfect municipal -- a gathering place, a social center and great golf. Or as golf pro Larry Lee, Sr. says, "This is a casual 'for the people' municipal golf course."

Golf Professional:
Larry Lee, Sr.

For further information:
Wailua Municipal Golf Course
P.O. Box 1017
Kapaa, Kauai, HI 96746
(808) 241-6666

KUKUIOLONO GOLF COURSE

Twenty miles from Lihue, there is a nice little challenge in the Kukuiolono Golf Course. Operating under a trust created by Walter D. McBryde, this nine hole course is a blessing for local residents and visitors in the know. It costs only $5.00 daily.

The fairways wind around ancient Hawaiian rock walls, over deep valleys and next to picturesque Japanese gardens. The layout is hilly and the 5th and 6th can get very windy. The "top of the hill" view is worth way more than you paid to play this gem. Fairways are common Bermuda and greens are not mowed every day but the course is challenging and lots of fun.

Most golfers use hand carts although carts are available. Remember this is leisure golf. The first nine is taken from the white, the second from the blue, making for 6,154 yards at par 72. "Due to the wind, it is best to play before 3:30 p.m.," says PGA golf pro, Toyo Shirai.

Golf Professional:
Toyo Shirai

For further information:
Kukuiolono Golf Course
P. O. Box 987
Lihue, Kauai, HI 96766
(808) 332-9151

MOLOKAI

KALUAKOI HOTEL AND GOLF CLUB

Kaluakoi Golf Course is one of Hawaii's great golf secrets, one not yet discovered by many tourists or local residents. Those who do know about it keep it to themselves.

Kaluakoi has well-manicured contoured fairways, glassy lakes and deliriously-placed bunkers. The views are spectacular and the beaches are the longest, whitest and cleanest in the Hawaiian Islands. On the back nine, deer, pheasant, wild turkey, quail and partridge will occasionally liven up your game.

A bad slice off the first tee will land you on the beach. In fact, the 1st, 3rd, 4th, 10th and 11th holes all run next to the beach. Course architect Ted Robinson must have enjoyed designing a course with all the natural ingredients already in place.

The dramatic 10th hole runs parallel to a rocky shore and is called "Hawaii's Pebble Beach." It is a 370-yard par 4 dogleg left. You tee off from a cliff toward a green some 150 feet below. Check the yardage on this hole -- it is longer than you think!

Kaluakoi offers a variety of experiences to challenge your game and whet your appetite for more.

Director of Golf:
Ben Neeley

For further information:
Kaluakoi Golf Course
P. O. Box 26
Maunaloa, Molokai, HI 96770
(808) 552-2739

IRONWOOD GOLF COURSE

Situated on the windward side of Molokai is a little gem of a golf course. Ironwood is a 2,790-yard par 35 nine holes developed in the 1930's by plantation workers for their own recreation, and recently given a new facelift.

The course is hilly, the fairways are narrow and tree-lined and the greens are small, fast and heavily guarded by bunkers. In late afternoon, winds pick up considerably, so plan to play in the morning.

For further information:
Ironwood Hills Golf Course
Del Monte, Molokai, HI 96757
(808) 567-6121

LANAI

Lanai, known as the "Pineapple Island," is a short distance from the tourist mecca of Maui. Hawaii's second smallest island, Lanai is only 13 miles wide by 18 miles long, with ground elevations from sea level to more than 3,400 feet. The island offers spectacular landscapes of red lava cliffs, green mountains and miles of pristine, secluded beaches.

Until recently, this isolated island of 2,300 inhabitants remained in a past era with heiaus (temples), petroglyphs, shipwrecks, cattle and pineapples. Lanai City was the only town, Lanai City Hotel was the only place to stay and the Cavendish Golf Course, a nine-hole, 3,071-yard par 36, was the only place to play.

In 1990, Lanai changed dramatically with the opening of two world-class resorts, The Lodge at Koele and The Manele Bay Hotel. The Lodge at Koele is in the style of an English country estate. The ocean-front Manele Bay Hotel overlooks Hulopoe Bay and has an architectural style reminiscent of Hawaii in the 1920's.

Adjacent to these resorts are two world class golf courses. The Experience at Koele course was designed by none other than Australia's "Great White Shark," Greg Norman and golf course architect Ted Robinson. The second eighteen, The Challenge at Manele, was designed by Jack Nicklaus.

The Experience at Koele is a compellingly beautiful mountain course, carved out of forested green hills and steep valley gorges and offering a challenging round of golf amid nature's finest scenery.

The Challenge at Manele makes the most of a magnificent oceanside setting. Dramatic over-the-water holes will test the mettle of even the finest players by demanding accurate and well-hit golf shots.

With the opening of these two new courses, the island of Lanai joins the ranks of premier golf destinations in Hawaii.

Set amidst the soaring pines and plunging ravines of Lanai's mountainous upcountry, Greg Norman's **Experience at Koele** is ranked among the best courses in America. And Jack Nicklaus' latest course, the **Challenge at Manele** is a masterpiece carved from lava cliffs 150 feet above the crashing surf. Players at either course may retire to the opulent old world comforts of the **Lodge at Koele** or the richly appointed Mediterranean elegance of the **Manele Bay Hotel** at seaside.

Golf packages start at $597.50 per person. For reservations or information, contact your travel agent or call our Central Reservations office at **1-800-321-4666**.

LANA'I
HAWAII'S PRIVATE ISLAND

"I NEVER BELIEVED IN A LEVEL PLAYING FIELD."
— GREG NORMAN

The Experience At Koele

The Experience at Koele, on the island of Lanai, is the first golf course in the United States designed by Australian professional golfer Greg Norman. And, since opening for play in 1991, few courses anywhere have generated as much excitement and applause as The Experience.

When Norman first saw the extraordinary highland site selected, he knew that the place and time had come to build his first 18-hole championship golf course in the United States.

"I wanted to wait for just the right one . . . the one that would allow me to contribute something really spectacular to the world of golf," Norman said.

Together with architect Ted Robinson, Norman has created a rugged yet compellingly beautiful golf course carved out of forested green mountains, steep valley gorges and windswept high plains. The par 72 course measures 7,014 yards from the back tees, 6,628 yards from the blues. Golfers will be treated to panoramic cross channel vistas of Maui and Molokai, occasional sightings of Axis deer that outnumber the human population, wild turkeys skittering across fairways, and dramatic changes in elevation.

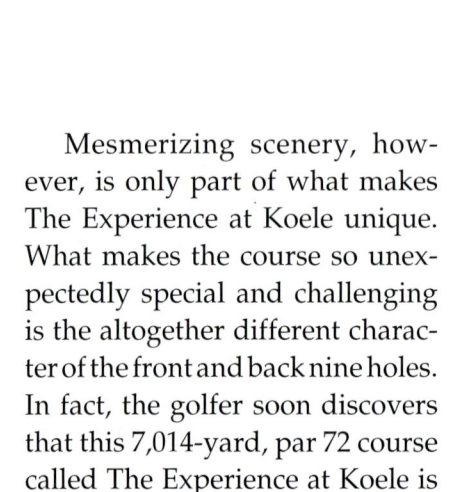

Mesmerizing scenery, however, is only part of what makes The Experience at Koele unique. What makes the course so unexpectedly special and challenging is the altogether different character of the front and back nine holes. In fact, the golfer soon discovers that this 7,014-yard, par 72 course called The Experience at Koele is really two completely different golf courses in one.

The front nine is situated in the island's central highlands, over 2,000 feet above sea level. It weaves its way through a cool mountain valley surrounded by giant pine and eucalyptus trees before it plunges down to the back nine on a vast windswept plain that overlooks the Pacific.

The "Experience" begins with a ride up a very steep cart path that winds its way up the side of a mountain to the first hole. Early morning, with fog still lingering in the treetops, is the best time to tee off. The cool clean mountain air is refreshing and stimulating.

Accuracy, more than distance, is the key to scoring well on the front nine. Thick rows of 80-foot tall Norfolk pines and deep rough line the narrow fairways, ready to swallow up errant drives. Also, deft iron play is a must to hit in regulation the small but well-manicured bent grass greens that are fast and true. This is the first golf course in Hawaii to have bent grass greens. To accomodate golfers of all skill levels, there are four sets of tees to choose among.

The back nine features wider, open fairways and larger greens. However, on the back nine, there are more water hazards and treacherous fairway and greenside bunkers. Also, the back nine plays a bit longer, as tricky tradewinds have a way of raising the difficulty factor a few notches.

Sudden and dramatic change in elevation and environment is what separates The Experience at Koele from any golf course, anywhere. It's an entirely new experience in golf course design and redefines how enjoyable and satisfying a game of golf can be.

Apparently, the experts agree. The Experience at Koele was named one of 1991's "Top Ten New Resort Courses" by <u>Golf Magazine</u> and "Best New Golf Course" by <u>Fortune</u> magazine. The course is now the site of the nationally-televised Merrill Lynch Shoot-Out Championship.

The Experience at Koele facilities include an attractive clubhouse with locker rooms, an executive

Greg Norman's design for The Experience at Koele carves 7,014 yards out of forests, gorges and upcountry plains.

putting course and a pro shop carrying the best-known names in golf apparel and equipment.

The adjacent Lodge at Koele is designed as a small, charming English country manor. The Lodge has a seaside sister property, the Manele Bay Hotel. Special rates are available for hotel and lodge guests.

Head Professional:
Marc Orlowski

For further information:
The Experience at Koele
P.O. Box 774
Lanai City, Lanai, HI 96763
(808) 565-4600

The Challenge At Manele

Christmas Day, 1993, brought a new golfing gift to Hawaii -- The Challenge at Manele. This course, which combines a breathtaking oceanside location with the distinct course architecture of golf's Golden Bear (Jack Nicklaus), is an experience you won't want to miss.

The Challenge at Manele is a par 72, links style eighteen with five tee positions, ranging from the black tees at 7,012 yards to the reds at 4,768 yards. The blue tees measure 6,086 yards.

The Challenge is the second course on the island, and is meant as a complement to The Experience at Koele, the upcountry course designed by Greg Norman and Ted Robinson.

Built on lava outcroppings along Lanai's southern coastline, the course winds through stands of native kiawe (mesquite) and ilima trees and a number of archaeological sites, some of which date from pre-contact times. The layout " . . . lets the course evolve in harmony with the existing landscape," said Nicklaus.

Three holes run parallel to the cliffs at Kuopoe Bay, so the Pacific Ocean is your oversized water hazard. Fairways are Tifway and greens are planted with Tifdwarf grass, a hybrid bermuda.

The Challenge at Manele, with its beautiful location, is kind on the eyes. But The Challenge is far less kind to errant golf shots. It is a "target" course, meaning if you land within the target area, you're fine; if you don't, you are out of luck. With many holes positioned only 50 yards back from the ocean, with drives from island cliffs over pounding surf or over natural gorges and ravines, with well-bunkered fairways hemmed in by rough that is truly rough -- you will have plenty of opportunity to demonstrate your skill in the accuracy department, particularly if you're playing from the back tees.

The configuration of the front nine is rather unusual, in that there are three par 3's and three par 5's. Front nine par is still 36 at the turn.

The 2nd hole presents your first real challenge on The Challenge. A par 4 measuring 398 yards from the blue tee, this hole requires two carries across ravines. On your drive, your carry to the target area is over a deep ravine filled with woods and scrub. The carry on your approach is over a shallower ravine, likewise filled with rough scrub and rocks. The green is relatively even, with breaks toward the setting sun. The green has a dramatic rock formation to the rear that should not come into play.

The 9th hole is a long 492-yard par 5, but it plays shorter since it is on a downslope from tee to green. If there is any wind at all, it will most likely be at your back, shortening the hole further. You will again have to carry twice: a natural area just in front of the tee boxes and, on your second shot, a deep ravine. For the big hitter who is reasonably accurate, the green is reachable in two.

On the back side, the demands for accuracy increase. The 12th is Manele's signature hole, a par 3 with tee boxes on one cliff, the green on another, the ocean aboil 150 feet below. While the distance is not that formidable -- it's 200 yards from the back tee, 145 yards from the blue -- this hole is psychologically intimidating as you tee up with nothing but ocean between you and what appears to be an overly small green. If there is wind, it will be blowing right to left, toward the ocean.

Once across the cove, the landing area is fairly broad. Play it to the right to catch the natural slope of the dogleg toward the hole.

Skills needed on the 17th shift from distance to accuracy on your approach shot. The green is wide, but shallow. You will need a seven or eight iron with backspin to place your ball properly. Should you overshoot, the ocean awaits!

The new clubhouse is now open and features a restaurant and bar.

The adjacent Manele Bay Hotel overlooks the beach at Hulopoe Bay. The hotel has an upcountry sister property, The Lodge at Koele. Special rates are available for hotel and lodge guests.

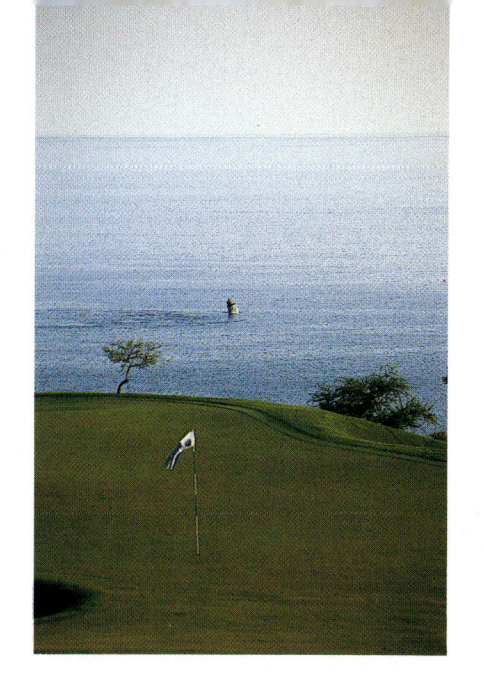

Head Professional:
Rob Nelson

For further information:
The Challenge at Manele
P.O. Box L
Lanai City, Lanai, HI 96763
(808) 565-2222

Carved into jagged lava cliffs high above the crashing surf of the Pacific, Jack Nicklaus' **Challenge at Manele** is the spectacular new target course along the southern coast of Lana'i. And if you're up to "The Challenge", you'll find an equally dramatic and formidable course amid the soaring pines and plunging ravines further inland; Greg Norman's extraordinary **Experience at Koele**. Players at either course may retire to the opulent old world comforts of the **Lodge at Koele** or the richly appointed Mediterranean elegance of the **Manele Bay Hotel** at seaside.

Golf packages start at $597.50 per person. For reservations or information, contact your travel agent or call our Central Reservations office at **1-800-321-4666**.

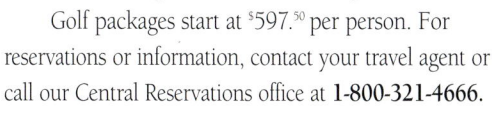

LANA'I
HAWAII'S PRIVATE ISLAND

"THE CHALLENGE IS
PLAYING IT.
OF COURSE BUILDING IT
WAS NO PICNIC."

— JACK NICKLAUS

GOLF HAWAII

The Complete Guide for Course Information & Tee Times

BIG ISLAND

Ali'i Country Club	(808) 322-2595
Discovery Harbor	(808) 929-7353
Francis H. I'i Brown Golf Course	(808) 885-6655
Hamakua Country Club	(808) 775-7244
Hapuna Golf Course	(808) 882-1035
Hilo Municipal Golf Course	(808) 959-7711
Kona Country Club	(808) 322-2595
Makalei Hawaii Country Club	(808) 325-6625
Mauna Kea Resort	(808) 882-7222
Naniloa Country Club	(808) 935-3000
Sea Mountain at Punalu'u	(808) 928-6222
Volcano Golf and Country Club	(808) 967-7331
Waikoloa Golf Club	(808) 885-4647
Waikoloa Village Golf Course	(808) 883-9621
Waimea Country Club	(808) 885-8777

KAUAI

Kauai Lagoons Golf & Racquet Club	(808) 241-6000
Kiahuna Golf Club	(808) 742-9595
Kukuiolono Golf Course	(808) 332-9151
Poipu Bay Resort Golf Course	(808) 742-9489
Princeville Makai Golf Courses	(808) 826-3580
Princeville Prince Golf Course	(808) 826-5000
Wailua Golf Course	(808) 241-6666

LANAI

Challenge at Manele	(808) 565-2222
Experience at Koele	(808) 565-4600

MOLOKAI

Ironwood Golf Course	(808) 567-6121
Kaluakoi Hotel and Golf Club	(808) 552-2555

MAUI

Kaanapali Golf Courses	(808) 661-3691
Kapalua Golf Club	(808) 669-8044
Makena Golf Courses	(808) 879-3344
Maui Country Club	(808) 877-0616
Pukalani Country Club	(808) 572-1314
Sandalwood Golf Course	(808) 242-4653
Silversword Golf Club	(808) 874-0777
Waiehu Municipal Golf Course	(808) 243-7400
Waikapu Golf Club	(808) 244-7090
Wailea Golf Course	(808) 879-2966

OAHU

Ala Wai Golf Course	(808) 296-4653
Bayview Golf Center	(808) 247-0451
Del Mar Golf School	(808) 695-5561
Hawaii Country Club	(808) 621-5654
Hawaii Kai Golf Courses	(808) 395-2358
Hawaii Prince Golf Club	(808) 944-4567
Honolulu Country Club	(808) 833-4541
Kahuku Golf Course	(808) 293-5842
Ko Olina Golf Club & Resort	(808) 676-5300
Koolau Golf Course	(808) 236-4653
The Links at Kuilima	(808) 293-8574
Makaha Valley Country Club	(808) 695-9578
Ted Makalena Golf Course	(808) 671-6480
Mid Pacific Country Club	(808) 261-9765
Mililani Golf Club	(808) 623-2222
Moanalua Golf Club	(808) 839-2411
Olomana Golf Links	(808) 259-7926
Pali Golf Course	(808) 261-9784
Pearl Country Club	(808) 487-3802
Royal Hawaiian Country Club	(808) 262-2139
Sheraton Makaha Resort	(808) 695-9544
Turtle Bay Country Club	(808) 293-8574
Waialae Country Club	(808) 732-1457
Waikele Golf Club	(808) 676-9000
West Loch Municipal Golf Course	(808) 676-2210